Kathleen Curtin
535 E. Kings College Dr.
Saint Johns, FL 32259

KEEPING GUARD

CHRISTY BARRITT

D1470420

River Heights

Copyright © 2019 by Christy Barritt

All rights reserved.

No part of this book may be reproduced in any form or by any electronic or mechanical means, including information storage and retrieval systems, without written permission from the author, except for the use of brief quotations in a book review.

COMPLETE BOOK LIST

Shadow of Intrigue

Storm of Doubt

Lantern Beach P.D.

On the Lookout

Attempt to Locate

First Degree Murder

Dead on Arrival

Plan of Action

Carolina Moon Series

Home Before Dark

Gone By Dark

Wait Until Dark

Light the Dark

Taken By Dark

Suburban Sleuth Mysteries:

Death of the Couch Potato's Wife

Fog Lake Suspense:

Edge of Peril

Margin of Error (coming soon)

Cape Thomas Series:

Dubiosity

Disillusioned

Distorted

Standalone Romantic Mystery:

The Good Girl

Suspense:

Imperfect

The Wrecking

Standalone Romantic-Suspense:

Keeping Guard

The Last Target

Race Against Time

Ricochet

Key Witness

Lifeline

High-Stakes Holiday Reunion

Desperate Measures

Hidden Agenda

Mountain Hideaway

Dark Harbor

Shadow of Suspicion

The Baby Assignment

The Cradle Conspiracy (coming soon)

Nonfiction:

Characters in the Kitchen

Changed: True Stories of Finding God through Christian Music (out of print)

The Novel in Me: The Beginner's Guide to Writing and Publishing a Novel (out of print)

Guard my life and rescue me; let me not be put to shame, for I take refuge in You.

—Psalms 25:20

*T*he cold rain felt like daggers penetrating Kylie Summers's skin. She tried to escape its torrent, but the drops kept chasing her, even as she retreated under the awning of the brick-fronted restaurant.

She pounded on the glass door again, desperate to get out of the storm. "Hello?"

The red neon sign above read The Revolutionary Grill. Yes, this was the place where her brother had instructed her to come to hide out. So where was Nate Richardson, her brother's best friend and the restaurant's owner? She shielded her eyes from the overhead streetlight and peered through the door. Inside, the place looked dead. Lights out, chairs on tables, staff gone.

It *was* almost midnight. She sighed and kicked the door. What now? She knew no one else in the historic town. She'd dropped her cell phone in a puddle of water two rest stops ago and she had exactly twenty-six dollars in her wallet.

A chill that had nothing to do with the weather crawled up her arms, an all too familiar feeling. She swung around, her wet hair slapping her in the face. She backed up against the rough brick wall that flanked the door. Her gaze frantically searched the black nighttime landscape.

Lightning streaked across the sky over the river beyond the parking lot. Thunder boomed. A lone pier stretched like a decrepit arm into the night. Lights from houses across the water stared at her.

Kylie pushed herself harder against the wall, wishing she could sink into it. Her gaze continued to dart across the landscape. What if the man who'd given her nightmares for the past six months was out there? The darkness and rain might cloak him, make him disappear. He could have followed her.

He always followed her.

Fear clenched her spine. Her breathing became rapid, uneven. She couldn't have another panic attack. Not now. Not here.

She had to find another entrance to this building. She had to figure out a way to find Nate. That, or she'd spend the night soaking wet in her car.

Nate had been expecting her to arrive three hours ago, a reasonable time for stores and businesses to still be open. But the treacherous weather had put her behind schedule, and he must have closed up shop and headed home for the night. She couldn't blame him.

March rain pelted her as she darted from the front of the building. Her foot sank into a deep puddle, splashing icy water up her pant leg. Her shivers intensified.

An alleyway lurked between the restaurant and gift shop next door. If she could cut through, maybe she'd find a back entrance to the grill.

Her throat went dry at the thought. Still, she had no choice.

Besides, the man couldn't have followed her here. She would have noticed.

Right?

She stepped onto the cobblestone street, dodging past trash cans, old buckets and a ladder.

She looked behind her. No one. Her heart continued to race.

Maybe all of this had been a bad idea. She should have stayed in Kentucky.

But she'd been hunted there and felt like a deer in the middle of an open field. No, her old life had to be put on hold. She couldn't continue living as she'd been for the past few months. Yet even here in Virginia she couldn't shake the feeling of unseen eyes watching her every move.

Pictures of the man flashed through her head in sync with the lightning around her. Pictures of his shadowed face, his hooded profile.

Her heart rate quickened. She tried to push the thoughts aside.

The end of the alleyway neared. She picked up her pace. Sheets of rain plastered her hair to her face.

She rounded the corner and spotted a black door with an alcove. She ducked into the space and pounded her fist against the door. *Please be there, Nate!* The thought of going through that alley again caused fear to slither up her spine.

She waited. The only sound she heard was that of the rain hitting the ground like bullets. Occasionally, thunder shook the air.

Nothing.

She knocked again. Why wasn't he answering?

She needed a Plan B. Only she didn't have one. She barely had a Plan A.

She clenched her eyes closed. How could one person control her life like this? Why did she let him have this power?

She waited in silence, hoping—praying—Nate had heard her.

He didn't. No one did. Not even God lately, it seemed.

She'd have to run back to her car, her only shelter. She could do that. She had to. Once protected behind locked doors, she'd figure out a plan. She took a tentative step into the rain.

A figure appeared around the corner from the alley. A hood concealed his face. A hood. It couldn't be . . .

He had found her.

The man who'd haunted her nightmares for months had finally caught her. Alone.

Nate Richardson spotted the woman at his back door. His relief instantly turned to a mix of worry and irritation. He'd been expecting her three hours ago, and she hadn't bothered to call or answer her cell phone. About thirty minutes ago, he'd called her brother, and now Bruce sounded ready to drive out to Virginia himself.

"Kylie." Nate stepped forward, keeping his hood over his forehead so his face would at least stay semidry.

The woman's eyes widened and she shrank back. "Stay away from me."

The rain poured onto his face, washing into his eyes. Nate stepped forward, trying to get out of the downpour. He needed to get her inside, to call her brother.

"I mean it! Stay back!" Her hands shot out in front of her.

"What are you—"

Before he could finish his sentence, Kylie darted across the parking lot.

Bruce had said his sister needed help. He didn't tell him that the woman was a mental case. What exactly had he gotten himself into by promising Bruce this woman could stay here and help him at his restaurant?

Nate watched her retreat for a moment while

contemplating his next move. Chasing her might further freak her out. But allowing her to run across the pothole-filled parking lot in this weather could cause her to twist an ankle or worse.

What would Bruce want him to do?

He sighed and began a steady jog to catch her. Rain sloshed in his face. He let his sweatshirt hood drop behind him. Rain soaked his clothing now, so the covering did him no good.

Nate saw Kylie glance back at him and then speed up. Her long hair appeared plastered to her blue blouse and her heels looked impossible to run in.

Then what Nate had feared would happen happened. Her body lurched forward and she sprawled on the asphalt.

He was only a few steps away from helping her. He quickened his pace.

Kylie turned toward him, panic clearly written in her wide eyes and oval-shaped mouth. "No! Stay away!" She tried to army-crawl forward, away from him.

The woman was a fighter. He'd give her credit for that. He just didn't know what she was fighting against.

"Kylie, stop freaking out. I just want to help."

"Stay away from me."

"Kylie, it's me—"

As soon as the words left his mouth, something hard came down across his head. His world began to spin and then went black.

ylie glanced at the white-haired woman who glared down at her while slapping a rolling pin in her hand. Kylie closed her eyes as tension drained away. Maybe God was watching out for her after all.

"Thank you," Kylie whispered, before realizing she couldn't be heard over the rainfall. She wiped some moisture from her face and said, a little louder, "Thank you!"

The woman continued to stare down at the man, knocked out flat on the ground, and shook her head. "I looked out my window and saw you being chased. I had to help."

Kylie gawked at the man, seeing his face for the first time since this whole ordeal began. She'd never imagined the man who'd given her so many night-mares would be handsome. In her mind, he'd had a long, crooked nose, tangled teeth, hollow eyes. This man had square, even features, sandy-colored hair. Kylie couldn't be sure in the darkness, but he might even be tanned.

She pulled her eyes away—at least she tried to. She needed to call the police. Let them know that this man should be arrested. Maybe she could finally live again. Go back to Kentucky. Focus on her business. Rebuild her life.

Kylie's attention turned to the woman with the rolling pin. She continued to stand over the man, shaking her head as if she pitied the poor soul who tried to mess with her. The woman might have white hair but obviously she had an iron will.

If only Kylie could be that strong.

The woman glanced at her with a perceptive gaze that made Kylie instantly trust her.

"I never thought Nate Richardson would be the type to do this," the woman said. "He always seemed like such a nice young man. Of course, I guess that's what everyone says about criminals."

Kylie sprang from the ground, adrenaline—and panic—rushing through each limb. "Nate Richard-son? Did you say Nate Richardson?"

"Why, yes, I did. Nate Richardson." The woman nodded down to the man. "He owns The Revolutionary Grill. I was making pies for tomorrow's dessert menu when I saw him chasing you. That's why I had my rolling pin handy. A good thing, huh?"

Kylie squeezed her eyes shut. What was wrong with her? Was she so paranoid that she'd just allowed her brother's best friend to be assaulted? She might as well just leave her bags in the car and find somewhere else to hide. This man wouldn't want her to be around anymore after this.

"Are you okay, dear?" The kindly, grandmother-like figure peered at her.

Kylie shook her head. "I'm afraid there's been a terrible misunderstanding. This man was trying to help me. I just didn't realize it."

"That sounds more like the Nate I know." The woman nodded, not appearing the least bit ruffled. "He seems tough on the outside but inside, he's sweeter than my shoofly pie."

Kylie's hand clamped over her mouth, muffling the urge to cry in horror or let her mouth drop open in shock. She had no idea what to do next. Or where to go. Or how to break the news to her brother, Bruce.

"Let's get him out of the rain until he regains

consciousness." The woman tucked her rolling pin under her arm and bent down as if she were going to haul him away herself.

Yes, they did need to get him out of the rain, but just how they'd do that perplexed Kylie. The man probably weighed two hundred pounds. The rolling pin mercenary couldn't weigh half that, even out in this storm soaking wet, and Kylie's own one hundred pounds wouldn't offer much help.

"I'm Darlene, by the way." The woman seemed to think better of pulling the man by herself and extended her hand toward Kylie.

Kylie shook it briefly. "My brother is a friend of Nate's. I'm Kylie."

"I just live right there." Darlene pointed to a white clapboard home only a few feet away. "So let's take him inside. I'll get my husband, Harvey, to help. It may take a moment. He'll have to put his dentures in first."

As the woman retreated inside, the rain began to taper.

Kylie knelt down beside Nate and flinched at the nasty bruise on his forehead. She should have known the man was Nate. But his hood had brought back so many bad memories. Fear had conquered her thoughts, as it often did lately.

Kylie closed her eyes. "I'm so sorry, Nate."

"You should be."

Her eyes snapped open in time to see Nate's eyelids flicker. He rubbed his forehead and attempted to sit up, the sudden lines around his eyes revealing his discomfort. Once he propped himself up on one elbow, his eyes narrowed at her.

"What's wrong with you? Kylie, I presume?"

Kylie opened her mouth, tried to form words. But how did one explain to a stranger the events of the last six months? How could she summarize the terror she'd felt without looking crazy?

"I know it will sound insane, but—"

"Wait till I tell the guys at Bible study about this." A man interrupted as he approached them, lumbering along beside Darlene, a huge grin stretched across his face. "Nate Richardson getting conked in the head by a girl."

Must be Harvey. Kylie looked closer. The man had teeth— nice, white, straight ones. He must have put his dentures in.

Darlene swatted him on the arm. "Harvey, don't give the boy a hard time. It's not his fault that I'm stealth-like."

"Stealth-like? You couldn't sneak up on an elephant. Beats me how someone who weighs so little can make so much noise stomping around the house all the time."

Harvey stuck his hand out to Kylie. "You must be the girl that Nate's fallen for."

"Just give me a hand, Harvey, and drop the comedy routine for a few minutes, will you?" Nate reached his hand up, grimacing at the movement.

Harvey still grinned as he pulled the broad ex-Coast Guardsman from the sopping ground. Nate's free hand still grasped his head and his eyes locked on Darlene and her rolling pin.

Darlene shook her head and raised her hands in the air in innocence. "Don't give me a dirty look. I was only trying to help the poor girl you were chasing. How was I to know it was a misunderstanding?"

"I just want to get out of this rain and lie down. Do you mind?" The commanding look in his eyes left little room for argument—from any one of the three.

Kylie shrank back and nodded. "Getting out of the rain sounds like a good idea to me, too."

Nate raised a finger as if he were going to lecture her, but then pressed his lips together and shook his head. "Right this way."

He took a step and stopped. His hands went to his temple.

"I better walk you back," Harvey said. "You need to go to the hospital?"

"No, I just need some aspirin and a rewind button."

"I can help with the aspirin but that's about it." Harvey squeezed his shoulder. "You'll have to get that rewind button from your magic genie."

He paused and pretended to rub an imaginary genie lamp.

Nate put his hand on Harvey's shoulder. "If only I had one, Harv."

Kylie wrapped her arms over her chest and tried to will her teeth to stop chattering. They wouldn't. Nor would her limbs stop shaking. This whole night was just too much. Yes, she'd take one of those rewind buttons also. If only they existed.

Nate knew he shouldn't snap at the woman. She hadn't been the one to hit him over the head with a rolling pin. But if Kylie had waited just a moment to have a logical conversation then maybe she would never have run away and caused this whole fiasco.

Still, he couldn't deny that Kylie looked just about as skittish as a cornered cat. Maybe he should have just let her run. Maybe he shouldn't have gone after her.

He sighed. He could do nothing about it now.

And man, his head was killing him. He'd never underestimate Darlene's brute strength again. Who knew the little woman who worked in the church nursery every Sunday could pack that much punch?

Thunder crashed again in the distance. The storm didn't want to let up. He had a feeling it was going to be a long, long night. A long week, for that matter, now that he'd have Kylie underfoot.

Was it only a week? How long had Bruce said she'd be here? For as long as needed until an investigation he was working on was over. Kylie was supposed to fill him in on the details.

If it had been any other friend, Nate would have said no. But not to Bruce. He could never say no to Bruce, especially not after Bruce had saved his life so many years ago. He was forever indebted to his friend.

He reached the alcove of his back door and stuck his key into the lock. He pushed the door open before turning to Harvey and Darlene. "I don't know whether to thank you or tell you I never want to see you again."

"You know you love us, Nate." Darlene smiled

sweetly, her rain bonnet reminding him a bit of a halo.

Yes, he did love them and knew they were only watching out for a woman in distress . . . distressed for some unknown reason.

He bid them good-night before sweeping his hand inside, motioning for Kylie to go in. Instead, she nodded toward the alley.

"I'll be going."

He raised his eyebrows. "Going where?"

"I'm not sure. But I understand that you probably don't want me here anymore after the headache I've caused you."

"You're not going anywhere."

The petite woman stopped and raised an eyebrow. He wasn't sure if the look in her eyes was relief or fire. Maybe a mix of both.

"Excuse me?" she finally said.

"I told your brother I'd watch after you. I plan on doing just that."

Her chin rose. "I don't need a babysitter. I just need a place to lie low for a few days."

Good, she'd said a few days. He could put up with her for a week, but no longer.

"Your apartment is already ready for you. It's no problem. If it was, I would have said no."

He climbed the stairs and listened to the sound of her shoes clicking on the wood, a much more pleasant sound than his heavy stomps.

Yep, just a few days. It was a good thing. The last thing he needed in his kitchen—or in his life—was a woman.

3

*H*ow could her brother ever have trusted this cranky man?

Their gazes locked, and Kylie knew this would be the longest week of her life. Yet at the same time, she couldn't help but feel relieved that she had a place to stay, somewhere to lie low until the madman back in Kentucky was arrested.

He would be arrested, right? The police had said they had a good lead and they should have the man behind bars within a matter of days. And with the man's advances becoming more aggressive, they'd suggested that Kylie get away until everything was cleared up.

She'd overcome obstacles before in her life—huge obstacles, she reminded herself. She could overcome this, also. Though it was the second time in her twenty-nine short years that she'd had to fight for her life, she'd learned a lot during that first battle.

Nate cleared his throat, and Kylie snapped from her thoughts to see him waving her through a doorway. She averted her eyes and stepped over the threshold into a modest apartment located over the restaurant that Nate owned. The small space would be perfect—for a week.

Her gaze swept the place. It appeared to have all that she needed—a great room with a breakfast bar separating the living room and kitchen, one bedroom and one bath. A wall of boxes lined one wall, no doubt storage items for the restaurant in the previously unused space.

"Home sweet home," Nate muttered, a sour expression still etched on his face.

Kylie swallowed before speaking. "I appreciate you giving me a place to stay. And I'm sorry for the rough start." She silently begged him not to ask for any more details. Not now.

He seemed to study her face for a moment before nodding. "I'll need you down in the kitchen by nine for prep. We open at eleven."

Kylie nodded. "No problem."

He rubbed his head and turned to leave, but paused to point toward the ceiling. "I'm in the upstairs apartment if you need me.

He stepped into the hallway, and Kylie had the impression that it was in her best interest that she not need anything in the next eight hours. Regardless, she cleared her throat. "Nate?"

He turned.

"You know you can't go to sleep after taking a blow like that, right?"

He scowled again. "Yeah, I know." He stomped toward the steps before yelling, "And call your brother. He's worried sick."

Kylie closed the door slowly and clicked each lock into place. She then leaned against the door and looked at her new temporary residence. She'd be safe here. No one knew where she'd gone except for her brother, and he'd never tell. Everyone else thought she was out doing research.

Her brother . . . she had to call him. She rushed across the room to where an old rotary phone rested on the breakfast bar and dialed the familiar number.

Bruce answered halfway through the first ring. "Where have you been? I keep trying to call your cell phone and it goes straight to voice mail."

His voice sounded tight and anxious—just what

Kylie had expected. "I know. I dropped my phone into a puddle on the way here. The weather put me behind schedule."

She twisted the phone cord around her index finger and shivered. The chill from her wet clothing seemed to seep through all the way to her bones. She'd have to get some dry clothes before going to bed.

"But you're there now? You found Nate?"

"Yeah, I'm here now." She glanced around the small apartment. "But I don't know about Nate. I think I'm just going to be in his way. And you know me, I like to do things my way."

"Yes, believe me, I know you." Her brother chuckled. "Listen, I know Nate comes across as tough, but once you get to know him, he's the nicest guy you'll ever meet. He'll make sure nothing happens to you."

Kylie raised an eyebrow as she remembered their introduction earlier. "I have my doubts."

"Kylie, believe me. You can trust Nate. I wouldn't have sent you there if you couldn't."

She didn't know who she could trust. And of all the people who came to mind, Nate Richardson sure wasn't one of them. Not with the cold reception she'd received from him. Not that she could blame him. He *had* been rendered unconscious because of her.

"Thanks for your help, big bro. You'll let me know as soon as he's arrested, right?"

"You'll be the first person to know. One of the officers here is a dead ringer for you. She's going to do the cooking demonstration on Friday, and we'll wait for your 'friend' to show up. Then we'll arrest him. We've got him on breaking and entering and harassment. This nightmare will be over soon. I promise."

Kylie closed her eyes and said a feeble prayer that things would go as planned. "Thanks, Bruce."

"Tell Nate I said hi. And Kylie? You *can* trust him."

She still wasn't sure about that. "Thanks."

She hung up and shivered again. She had to get some dry clothes.

She glanced out the window as lightning flashed across the nighttime sky. The last thing she wanted was to go outside again. Was the only way to get to her car through that dark alley again? There had to be another way. She bit her lip, considering her options.

Beneath her, a nice-size puddle had formed on the floor. She opened a door beside the bathroom, hoping to find some towels. Nothing. She frowned. She couldn't—or shouldn't, at least—complain. At least the place was furnished. But the furnishings would do nothing right now to keep her from catching a cold in her soaked clothing.

That settled it. She had to get to her car. She could ask Nate to go with her.

She shook her head, remembering his rotten mood and realizing she'd only further perturb him by disturbing him now. They'd already gotten off to a rough start.

As quietly as possible, she opened the door and tiptoed into the hallway. A wooden floorboard creaked underneath her, and she shushed it as she crept down the stairs. She paused at the outside door, trying to gather her courage before plunging into the night.

"Where do you think you're going?" Nate stood at the top of the steps and watched as Kylie gasped, turned around and pressed herself against the door with wide eyes. A hand went over her heart. The woman looked almost childlike with her big eyes and delicate features.

"You scared me to death." Kylie's hand moved from her heart to her forehead and she closed her eyes, looking as if she wanted to melt right then and there.

"Yeah, same here. I thought someone was trying to break in." He lumbered the rest of the way down the stairs, his head still throbbing. When would that aspirin kick in? "What are you doing? You have no business going out at this hour."

"I need my bags." She looked down at her clothes. "I've got to change or I'll end up sick and be no help to you at all."

It was true. Nate had already changed into some sweats and a T-shirt. He hated to go back out into that rain again. But he would, like it or not. His mother had raised him well.

He nodded the opposite way of the back door. "Come on. We'll go through the kitchen and avoid some of the storm outside."

He didn't check to see if Kylie was following him. He could hear her soft steps behind him, though. He unlocked the door leading to his kitchen and allowed her to go inside first.

She stopped in the doorway and her face lit up as she looked around. "This is fabulous."

Her compliment gave him a small amount of satisfaction. "Thanks. I like it."

She stepped forward and gingerly ran her finger across the tile counter. "You've kept this as original as possible to a Colonial times restaurant, haven't you? That's just brilliant."

Nate watched her carefully, surprised by her fascination and knowledge. "Yeah, I wanted to give people the experience of what it would be like to eat in Revolutionary War times—with a few modern amenities, of course. That's why they come to Yorktown, after all. To experience a bit of the past."

She twirled around, apparently forgetting about her wet clothes and whatever problems had brought her here. Her eyes seemed to absorb each and every appliance—or lack thereof. She looked like a girl who'd woken up on Christmas morning to find she'd gotten everything she'd asked for.

"This is going to be amazing."

Nate actually felt his lip begin to twitch in the start of a grin. Seeing someone who actually had some passion for the place felt nice. He only wished he had a touch of that same fire. "I'm glad you like it."

"I more than like it. I'm just . . . I'm amazed. Maybe being here won't be so bad after all."

The beginning of Nate's smile slipped into a frown. She seemed to catch what she said and she dropped her hand from the countertop to look at him with doe-like eyes. "Sorry."

"No need to apologize, Kylie." He stepped around her, going toward the front door.

If she didn't need to apologize, then why did he feel so annoyed? He knew the answer. He'd already screwed up one rescue mission and he had no intention of screwing up another. But Kylie—the very person he was trying to save—could very well be his biggest obstacle also.

Just as he reached the front door, lightning brightened the sky to purple. The flash of light illuminated a man at the restaurant's front window. The man stood with his hands to his eyes, peering through the glass into the darkness.

Before Nate could say a word, a splitting scream cut the air.

4

"Harvey," Nate mumbled, walking toward the door.

The tall, lanky man grinned and waved from outside, clueless to how shocking it had been to see his face pressed to the glass.

Nate unlocked the door and pushed it open. "All due respect, Harvey, but are you crazy?"

Harvey stepped inside, shaking the rain from his coat. His miniature poodle walked in behind him and followed suit, sending water all over the entryway.

"No, I'm not crazy. Your earlier fiasco, you know, the one where you drug me out of bed? Well, that woke up Tinker-bell and she insisted on coming outside in the rain for a little potty break. As I was walking past, I saw the light on and just wanted to make sure all was okay."

Nate glanced behind him at Kylie, who still stood with a ghost-white complexion. Her hands gripped the countertop, the skin tight over her knuckles. The woman was a basket case. He knew she needed to hide for a few days, that someone had threatened her. But he would need to find out more. *Terrified* seemed to be an understatement.

"Harvey, wait here with Kylie for a minute, will you?" He turned to Kylie. "Kylie, let me have your car keys so I can grab your stuff."

She nodded, fished through her pocket and pulled out a ring of keys. She tossed them to Nate, her hands trembling. She noticed him staring and quickly stuffed her fingers into her jean pockets.

With Kylie under Harvey's watchful eye, Nate jogged into the rain to her car—the only one in front of his restaurant at this hour. He popped the trunk and heaved out a large—very large—suitcase. This is how the woman packed for a few days?

He slammed the trunk closed and hauled the suitcase inside.

Harvey and Kylie were chatting like old friends when Nate stepped back into the restaurant. Kylie's face had lost some of its ashen appearance as she squatted, petting Tinkerbell. He noticed her hands still trembled, though.

She stood when Nate approached and leveled her gaze with his, seeming to retrieve some of her confidence. Nate dropped the suitcase in front of her, a little harder than he intended. "Dry clothes."

He chose not to mention that his were now soaking wet—again. Instead, he looked at Harvey. "Why don't you go out the back door, Harvey? You won't get quite as wet."

"Sounds good." Harvey winked at Kylie before turning to walk through the kitchen. "I'll see you tomorrow morning!"

"Tomorrow morning?" Nate questioned.

"I just invited you and Kylie over for breakfast. We've got to get to know our new neighbor. It's the Southern way."

Nate started to argue but changed his mind. "I'll see you then, Harvey."

He opened the door for his neighbor, watched as he exited and then turned, expecting to see Kylie behind him. She was gone.

Curiously, he wandered down the hall, through the kitchen and back into the dining area. By the front door, Kylie knelt with a roll of paper towels, wiping up the rain Harvey dripped inside.

"You don't have to do that, Kylie."

She glanced up, her face pale again. "It's okay. I don't mind. Besides, I need to earn my keep. Call me crazy, but it's the way I was raised."

He started to deny what she'd said but changed his mind. Instead, he grabbed some more paper towels and wiped at the wet footprints tracked across the floor.

After they finished cleaning, Nate touched Kylie's arm. She flinched.

"Listen, I know you're wet and tired. Will you do me a favor, though?"

She nodded. "Of course."

"Go upstairs, change and then come back down here, have some coffee and tell me what's going on. I can't help you if I'm in the dark."

She looked numb as she said, "Okay."

"Let me get your suitcase upstairs for you then."

Dressed in dry yoga pants, a sweatshirt and slippers, Kylie crept downstairs. Her gaze darted to every dark corner. She flinched at each creak of the old wooden staircase. Her heart sped as she paused by the backdoor.

How had her life become this? Just when she'd been doing so well, truly beginning to stand on her own feet. Then one man had decided to turn her world upside down.

She'd fought coming here, convinced herself that going into hiding made her look weak. She wanted to stay in Kentucky and confront her faceless nightmare head on. Her brother insisted staying in Kentucky wasn't safe. And after that last encounter with the person she called "the Man in Black," she'd conceded—but not happily.

She'd come to refer to him as the Man in Black because that was simply all she knew about her stalker. Not knowing what his face looked like only increased her anxiety. His eyes and features were always shadowed by that hood. He could be anyone.

Kylie had seen him only three times. Once he'd been outside the window at her house. Another time he'd been watching in the distance as she went grocery shopping. He hadn't gotten close to her, but she'd known it was him from the way he'd stood idly by, watching. And at her last cooking demonstration, he'd been there, at the back of the crowd. By the time she'd alerted someone, he'd disappeared, probably abandoning the sweatshirt so police couldn't identify him.

All she knew was that he was tall, broad-shouldered, relatively thin. On the phone, his voice sounded gravelly and low—probably disguised. In emails, he used proper English, which made Kylie think he had to be educated. On handwritten notes, his writing appeared calm, controlled—like he knew just what he was doing.

Kylie shuddered.

She'd been over a list of suspects with the police, but the list seemed so ambiguous. There was the fan who constantly left aggressive messages on the public online forum to her cooking show. Of course, the police could never trace the address, as the man seemed to use computers at various places around town, all without security cameras.

However, the stalker could be someone who'd given no clue to his identity—someone who'd watched her show and developed an obsession, someone who'd seen her shopping and she'd caught his eye. He could be a friend, a neighbor, an ex-boyfriend.

At the thought of an ex-boyfriend, Kylie squeezed her eyes closed. Colin was far too sophisticated and cultured to pull off a stunt like this. Besides, he'd avoided her since they broke up. Why would he avoid her in general and stalk her at every other time? Sure, he'd been controlling, but he would never go this far.

Would he?

They'd dated for a year before Kylie finally had the sense to break up with him. He was the president of a local advertising agency. She'd catered an event at his office and he'd immediately taken an interest in her. She'd been flattered and, initially, swept off her feet. His strength and advice had been comforting in the beginning. But as she got to know him, she realized that the more they were together, the more she was losing herself.

Slowly, he'd begun to isolate her from her friends and family. He'd begun to critique everything she did. He'd begun giving career advice and calling her producer to insist he make it happen. He'd even figured out her email password and begun answering her emails. He'd accepted invitations or declined opportunities without so much as a mention to Kylie. He'd claimed he was only trying to make her into the successful woman she had the potential to be, and in order to do so, she needed to align herself with certain people and write others out of her life completely.

The final straw came when she found out he was cheating on her. She wished she'd seen the signs earlier, that she'd gotten out before discovering his betrayal. The good thing, she comforted herself, was that at least she'd gotten out.

Despite his cheating, Colin hadn't taken the breakup well. Told her she'd realize her mistake and come running back.

She hadn't.

Instead, she'd avoided him whenever possible and comforted herself with her friends and family, who'd been terribly neglected. Life had finally started feeling normal and happy again.

Until her stalker showed up.

She braced herself to face Nate. She rounded the corner into the dining room, where Nate sat with two steaming mugs before him. The rain still pounded against the window as the storm raged outside.

Kylie took a minute to observe him as she approached. He really was a good-looking guy in a tough, outdoorsy type of way. As his arms rested on the table, she noticed the fine definition of his muscles peeking out from under his T-shirt. She scolded herself for even noticing.

Nate nodded her way when he spotted her in the doorway, thankfully not seeming to notice that she'd been staring. "Come on over and have a seat, Kylie."

Her slippers made no sound as she crossed the floor and sat across from Nate. He pushed a ceramic mug toward her. "It's decaf."

She wrapped her fingers around the warmth of the mug. "Thanks."

She normally used cream and sweetener, but tonight she'd drink it black. She sipped the bitter liquid.

"So, Kylie, I need you to tell me what's going on," Nate started. "I don't mind you staying here—I'm more than happy to help out you and your brother —but I need to know more about the circumstances bringing you here."

How did she tell him without causing him to overreact? Of course, with everything that had already happened since she arrived, him overre-acting could be a forgone conclusion. "How much did Bruce tell you?"

"Just that he was fearful for your safety. He told me you would fill in the rest of the blanks."

She'd have to give her brother credit for that. It must have killed him not to go into detail, but that's what Kylie had requested. She wanted to handle this mess on her terms, as much as possible, at least.

She sucked in a breath. "The rest of the story would be that a man has been following me—

stalking me, I suppose—for the last several months. Recently, he's become more aggressive. It's become more and more apparent that this man has no intention of backing off. The police finally collected enough evidence to press charges, but first they have to figure out whom to press charges against. My brother is working with the police to set up a sting and make that happen. I just need to lie low until everything settles."

She looked away and took a sip of coffee.

"Are you sure he didn't follow you here?"

The thought caused fear to grip her heart as the emotion had done several times already this evening. "I'm not sure of anything, Nate. My brother is the only one who knew I was coming here. I didn't even tell my best friend or boss. I took back roads on my way here. I didn't see any signs of anyone following me. But this man always seems to be a step ahead of me."

"And you have no idea who he is?"

She shook her head. "No idea. I've never seen his face."

"Which is why you freaked out when you saw me approaching you with my sweatshirt hood up . . ."

She nodded and glanced at the knot already

forming at his temple. "I'm sorry about that. Is your head okay?"

His eyes darkened. "I'll be fine." He leaned back in his chair and took a breath. "You know anything about working in a restaurant, Kylie?"

"A restaurant? No, not terribly much. But I have experience as a cook."

He cocked an eyebrow and waited for her to explain.

Was this the time to tell Nate about her cooking show back in Kentucky? Or about the successful catering business that she and her friend had started? No, she decided. She'd have time to share that later. Right now, her head pounded and she needed some time alone.

She stood. "I'll explain tomorrow. I promise you have nothing to worry about. I may not have restaurant expertise, but I've got plenty of experience. But before I get into that, I could really use some sleep."

In her room, Kylie pulled the covers up tight around her neck. Despite adding another layer of clothing, shivers still racked her body. Was the weather causing her chills? Or could it be everything that had happened?

She pushed her face into her pillow, remembering what a fiasco tonight had been. The fact that someone had intimidated her enough for her to go running sent a flare of anger up her spine—at herself and her stalker. She fought against anyone dictating what would happen with her, preferring to make her own decisions. But now she found herself in this situation.

Thunder rolled outside. She pulled the covers up to her eyes.

Soon enough, all this would be over. Her brother had promised her. She expected a call sometime this week saying that her stalker had been arrested and she could go back home and resume her normal life.

She sighed and turned over in bed. Would her life ever be normal again? Or would she always jump at every shadow, tense at every unknown sound? She bit her bottom lip, hoping that wouldn't be the case. She'd overcome other obstacles in her life—big obstacles. She could overcome this also.

As thunder grumbled again outside, Kylie realized she shouldn't have drunk that coffee, even if the brew was decaf. Despite how tired she'd felt downstairs, her mind felt fully alert right now. She glanced at the clock beside her bed. 3:23 a.m.

She pressed her head back into the pillow, wishing sleep would find her. Instead, her thoughts raced, replaying her drive here.

Could she really be certain that no one had followed her? She'd continuously checked her rearview mirror for headlights. At times on the road, she knew no one was behind her. That meant no one could be trailing her, right? She had no reason not to feel safe here.

Her heart slowed some.

She sat up and flicked the light on. She had to distract herself from these thoughts before she went crazy. From the floor, she grabbed her oversized purse, reached into it and pulled out a paperback novel.

Reading always relaxed her. This particular book was a romance novel. Just the thing to distract her from her troubles.

She leaned back into her pillows and opened the first page.

She gasped.

Written across the inside cover, in fat red marker, were the words "Kylie, I'll always be watching you."

5

*N*ate's eyes drooped with sleepiness as he rapped on Kylie's door at seven the next morning. He'd downed two cups of decaf and three cups of full-strength coffee last night to make himself stay awake. Good for his possible concussion but bad for his mental health.

He hadn't been able to get Kylie Summers's porcelain face and delicate figure out of his mind throughout his sleepless hours. He didn't know what he'd expected of his best friend's sister, but not the beautiful woman who'd shown up three hours late with rain plastering her chestnut hair to her face and wide, imploring eyes.

He rapped at her door again, harder this time.

"Coming." The word couldn't have been said

with much less enthusiasm.

Nate shifted his weight until Kylie finally pulled open the door. The circles under her eyes showed him that she clearly hadn't gotten much more sleep than he had. But she still looked beautiful, even in jeans and a long-sleeved pink T-shirt.

"Morning." She barely smiled as she reached over to grab her coat from the couch.

Nate stuffed his hands into his pockets, unsure of exactly what to say to his new boarder. "Morning, Kylie. Rough night?"

"You could say that."

"Too much on your mind?"

She reached back inside the apartment and fumbled with something before finally revealing a book. She shoved the paperback toward him and frowned. "Open it."

He did as she said. His eyes widened at the roughly written words on the inside cover. "You just found this?"

"No, I found the message last night as I tried to relax before going to bed."

"Hence your sleepless night." He stared at the words, personalized to Kylie so she could make no mistake they were written for her. "When did you get this book?"

She answered immediately, probably because she'd been replaying all those events during her sleepless night. "Right before I left for this trip. I bought it at the grocery store and stuck it in my purse."

"Did you go anywhere after that?"

She shrugged. "I stopped by work for a few minutes to pick up some papers and then I had dinner with my brother."

"Any opportunities for someone to access your purse?"

"Apparently." She shrugged, sounding defeated. "It makes no sense."

"I'm sorry, Kylie. I know this guy has got you shaken up."

"He's right, you know. He is always watching me. He must have been waiting until just the right moment when he could grab the book from my purse and send me that message." She tossed the book back onto the dinette and raised her eyebrows in conjunction with her sigh.

Nate couldn't help but think she looked like she bore the weight of the world. "It doesn't matter now, I guess. What matters now is that we go eat breakfast."

"I know Harvey and Darlene will be a nice

distraction from everything. They always are. Full of surprises."

"I would have guessed that." Her face registered a slight but genuine smile.

The two walked silently down the steps and out the back door. A brisk wind greeted them, matching the gray day. Kylie's gaze roamed the parking lot behind his restaurant.

"So, this is Yorktown?"

Nate shrugged. "Well, this is a public parking lot for Yorktown. The rest of the town is there on the waterfront or on the bluff to the south." He pointed to the blocks of historic houses. "There's some great stuff to see around here if you like history."

"It was always one of my best subjects in school." She stuffed her hands into her coat pockets as they journeyed across the parking lot toward Harvey's house. "I'll have to take some time to explore, if I have the chance. Of course, I may not be here long enough."

It sounded like they were both praying for the same thing.

They reached the house, which also served as a bed-and-breakfast, and Nate rang the doorbell. He knew the couple didn't have any guests at the time. Immediately, Tinkerbell began barking inside.

Sometimes Nate was convinced that the couple would never know anyone was at their door if it weren't for that dog. Neither of them had the best hearing these days.

Harvey opened the door and the scent of bacon drifted out. As if on cue, Nate's stomach grumbled. He'd always been a sucker for Darlene's cooking. Her food reminded him of his mother's—only better, which he never admitted out loud.

"Come in, come in," Harvey extended his arm behind him, welcoming them inside. "You got here just in time. The pancakes are just coming off the griddle."

"Smells wonderful." Kylie reached for Harvey's hand. He grabbed it and, instead of shaking it, placed a kiss there. Nate carefully watched Kylie's reaction. She didn't seem taken aback by the action, thankfully. In fact, she smiled. Harvey had always been a charmer.

Darlene appeared from around the corner wearing a checkered blue-and-white apron, holding her now famous rolling pin in one hand. Nate's head throbbed just looking at it. "Welcome! I'm so glad you're both joining us. Kylie, I look forward to finding out all about you."

They were ushered into the dining room and

promptly seated. If only the waitresses at Nate's restaurant would be this prompt and welcoming, then maybe he'd get some more business. Of course, some people might say the same thing about his food. If it tasted like Darlene's, people would be standing in line to eat at his place.

"Everyone recovering okay from last night?" Darlene stared at them with sweet, unblinking eyes. Her hands were clasped in front of her, as if at any time she might clap joyfully.

Kylie nodded. "I'm hanging in. My arrival didn't exactly go the way I'd planned. I do apologize again for the way everything played out yesterday."

"I'm sure your actual arrival was much more exciting than you could have planned. It's good to add some excitement to your life sometimes." Darlene grinned and giggled. Finally, she used those posed hands to actually clap. "Well, let's eat before the food gets cold."

Harvey offered up a prayer and then Darlene brought out banana pancakes with cream-laced syrup, maple bacon and a festive fruit salad.

Kylie's eyes lit up on the first bite of pancake. "This is fabulous, Darlene. Truly amazing."

Harvey winked. "She's one great cook, isn't she?"

"Darlene makes all the desserts for the restaurant," Nate informed her.

"Well, you need to keep her around. That's for sure." Kylie nodded and took another bite of pancake, her eyes closing in what looked like pure delight.

Harvey and Darlene began to talk about an upcoming church social, a visit from their grandkids in the summer and changes in the Fife and Drum of Yorktown. Nate listened, relieved to not have to talk. He preferred listening, most of the time.

Kylie had warmed up to the couple quickly. She asked lots of questions, nodded, laughed. She actually seemed halfway normal. Maybe her stay here wouldn't be a total headache.

At nine o'clock, Nate stood and announced they needed to go and begin prepping the kitchen for the lunch crowd.

Kylie nodded and rose. "Thank you so much for having us. I really enjoyed your food and would love the recipes."

"I'd love to pass them on to you." Darlene hugged Kylie. "Now, you come back and see us again before you leave, you hear? And don't let Nate work you too hard."

Kylie glanced at him. "I won't."

Nate wasn't sure about that. He knew one thing: the busier he kept her, the less she'd think about her stalker or have the chance to get in trouble.

By the time the lunch crowd began to wander in, Kylie had chopped every vegetable imaginable, sorted through various lunch meats and prepared two different kinds of soup. She'd also reviewed the menu multiple times with Nate, not overly impressed by his selections, which were vast. Too vast, truly, for a restaurant like this. She kept quiet, though. She wasn't here as a consultant, nor had he asked her opinion.

"You never did tell me if you had experience working in a restaurant," Nate said in between explaining how to make maple-glazed chicken. "You seem to know what you're doing."

"I have my own cooking show back at home. It's nothing huge, and I'm by no means famous, but I do cook in front of a camera for viewers every week. It's a great job. I also have my own catering business."

"You'll have to tell me more about it sometime. It sounds interesting." Nate walked to the freezer and pulled out a container of something. "Right now, I need to explain these crab cakes."

Kylie blinked. "They're frozen?"

"I make them ahead and freeze them. Saves a lot of time."

Kylie nodded, deciding not to interject her opinion as Nate showed her how the cakes were prepared. When he finished, Kylie glanced at her watch and saw they were close to opening. "So, when do the cooks get here?"

Nate scowled and wiped the cast-iron stove top one more time. The appliance was spotless. "I am the cook."

Kylie nodded, choosing her words carefully. "I thought you managed the restaurant?"

"I manage the restaurant and cook. Just like the hostesses are always the waitresses also. We're not a big place, so we all have to wear multiple hats."

Kylie bit her lip. No, she'd never run a restaurant, but Kylie knew enough to know Nate needed more help. She did have experience running a successful catering business, so she knew how to manage people, how to develop recipes that would satisfy crowds, how to make her staff feel appreciated.

Still, Kylie couldn't waltz in, criticize Nate's work and then be on her merry way. So she'd stay quiet, no matter how miserable it made her. She didn't like to be told what to do, so she certainly didn't want to offer unsolicited advice to others.

Their first order came in, and both Nate and Kylie got busy. And quiet. Neither of them said anything, except for Kylie to occasionally ask questions about an order, or for Nate to state how to prepare a dish properly.

Kylie felt at home in the kitchen. She always had. She loved coming up with new recipes or new takes on old recipes. But the food she prepared today was mindless. Sandwiches, soups, salads. Nothing exciting. Nothing revolutionary.

It didn't matter. This wasn't her restaurant, she reminded herself again.

After the lunch crowd left, Nate moseyed out front to talk with someone who appeared to be a regular customer. One of the waitresses came back to introduce herself to Kylie.

"I'm Suzy." The woman was probably in her midtwenties with a sharp wedge hairdo that was black on the bottom and bright red on top. She had multiple earrings in both her ears and tattoos instead of jewelry around her fingers and wrists. "Good to have you here."

Kylie wiped her hands on a white dish towel and

reached for Suzy's hand. "I'm Kylie. I'm just filling in here for a few days, trying to get some restaurant experience."

Her words weren't a lie. She did want experience. She didn't want anyone else to know the real life-or-death reasons behind her being here. Only Nate. Her brother had said she could trust Nate, and she was going to have to take him at his word.

Suzy set her tray on the counter, as if prepared to stay awhile and talk. "Well, I know Nate could use the help."

Kylie prepared a glass of water for herself and decided to take a break. She took a sip and stood across from Suzy. "You guys have a small staff."

"Things have been tight, so Nate tries to watch every dime. I tried to tell him there are some things you just shouldn't cut back on. He doesn't listen."

Kylie nodded. "He seems pretty . . ."

"Gruff?" Suzy laughed, obviously not shy about sharing her opinion. "You don't have to beat around the bush with me. Yeah, he comes across as a little grumpy sometimes. Deep inside, he's not. I think the stress of owning this restaurant has just taken its toll on him."

Kylie leaned against the counter, intrigued to find out more about her temporary boss. "You make it sound like he doesn't want to own this place."

"The restaurant was handed down to him from his father. Nate never wanted to own it, but I'll give him credit, he's tried to make the best of it. There's rumor that the place might go up for sale soon, though. If Nate has his way, he won't own this place very much longer."

Kylie pulled her chin back in surprise. "Up for sale? I had no idea."

"Yeah, he doesn't tell many people about it. I think he's afraid of disappointing some of his father's old friends."

"Darlene and Harvey, by chance?"

"Yes. You've met them?"

Kylie nodded. "A couple of times already."

"Yeah, so all of that combined with the bad relationship he just got out of a few months ago—"

"Kylie." Both women snapped their heads toward Nate, who'd appeared in the doorway dangling a telephone. How much of the conversation had he heard? "You have a phone call. Your brother."

Suzy scurried away, no doubt before she heard an earful from her boss. Kylie had no choice but to approach Nate, though. She couldn't read his expression as she took the phone and placed it at her ear.

His gaze remained on her another moment before he turned and stomped back into the dining room.

Once he was out of earshot, she finally spoke into the receiver. "I thought I already called you and told you I was here and doing okay. Are you doing the overprotective thing on me again?" She tried to sound lighthearted and erase all the worry that always seemed to be present in her brother's voice.

"Kylie." His voice sounded serious, much more serious than she'd expected. "Your house was ransacked last night."

"Ransacked? What do you mean? I thought the police were watching it." That ice-cold feeling chilled her spine again. She backed away from the dining area, out of earshot.

"A cruiser was going past every ten minutes. We have no idea how the break-in happened. It almost seems like someone was watching, like they knew we were monitoring the house and waited until just the right moment to strike."

"Was anything taken?"

"It's hard to say. Nothing valuable. Your TV, computer, jewelry, all of those things are still there."

"So . . ." Kylie couldn't finish her thought. Her mind raced with possibilities.

Her brother's voice softened. "No, this doesn't

appear to be a random break-in. This was mostly likely your stalker, and he's most likely trying to figure out where you went." Her brother paused. "Did you leave anything in your house that might give away your location, Kylie?"

Had she? Her mind replayed the events of the past few days. The only place she'd written down her destination was in her notebook. She'd jotted Nate's address and phone number, plus some quick directions her brother had given her. But then she'd torn that page out and had brought it with her. That paper had sat in the car seat beside her on the drive here. She was sure of it.

"No, I didn't leave anything there."

"Good. You should still be safe there in York-town. Did you let Nate know what's going on?"

"We talked last night."

"If anything at all suspicious happens, let him know. Promise me?"

"I promise." Before they hung up, Kylie told him about the note she'd found scribbled in her book.

Her brother's voice sounded stern. "Kylie, be careful. I don't like this."

She nodded. "Neither do I."

6

*N*ate looked away from a conversation with one of his regulars and glanced at Kylie, whose face looked whiter than flour. She slowly placed the phone on the hook, and from the way her body sagged, it looked like she hung on to the wall mount to keep from sinking to the floor. He had the urge to go and help steady her, but he didn't. She seemed to like her privacy, and Nate wanted to respect that, even if he had to grip the chair to keep himself from rising.

But when Kylie looked over at Nate with strained eyes, he decided she was inviting him to help. He apologized to his customer as he hastily rose and walked into the kitchen. Kylie appeared dazed as he approached.

"Everything okay?" He slapped the dish towel over his shoulder, trying not to appear too concerned. Still, he reached out and gripped her elbow so she wouldn't stumble.

Her eyes flickered around as if her brain was processing a large amount of information. "Someone broke into my apartment back in Kentucky last night."

He bristled at the news. "The same man?"

"Most likely. Nothing was stolen."

"Your brother is a good police officer, Kylie. I know he's making sure that the people assigned to your case are doing their job. They'll figure out whoever is doing this to you. And when they do, that person will pay."

Kylie nodded. "You're right. It's just so hard being here when all of that is happening back home. I feel like I need to be there, to go through my things, help pick up the pieces."

He squeezed her elbow, trying to reassure her. "You'll have plenty of time for that later, Kylie. Right now you just have to focus on your safety. That's the most important thing."

She let out a little laugh, the action ruffling her bangs. "You sound like my brother, you know."

Nate smiled and released his grip on her some. "Your brother is a good man."

She sighed and leaned against the counter, some of the lines disappearing from her face. "He said you served together in the Coast Guard."

"That's right. Bruce helped keep me sane." He did more than that. Bruce had saved Nate's life. After a devastating rescue gone wrong, Nate had picked up some bad habits to ease his pain. Bruce had been the only one brave enough to gently, yet firmly, correct Nate. He couldn't imagine what life might be like today if Bruce hadn't intervened.

"When did you guys work together?"

"When we were stationed at Elizabeth City, North Carolina. We were both rescue swimmers. The first day we met we discovered we both rooted for the same pro football team. We were inseparable after that."

Kylie pulled her arms across her chest. "I used to pray for Bruce every day when he did that job." She closed her eyes. "Jumping out of helicopters, battling the seas, the temperatures and storms and all those other elements that came with being out in the middle of the ocean . . . I don't know how you guys did it."

Those were the moments that Nate missed.

Those rushes of adrenaline. Knowing he could save someone's life. Using every ounce of strength to do his job.

But there had been tough moments also, moments when he hadn't been able to save everyone. Moments where he had to tell one family member that another hadn't made it. He pushed the memories away.

Saving people—whether it had been at sea or just in life itself—had been his passion. He'd failed. And as further proof and a daily reminder of that failure, he now ran this restaurant.

"Nate?"

Kylie's voice pulled him out of the memory. He decided to put the focus on Bruce and hoped Kylie wouldn't ask too many questions of him. He wasn't ready to go there. The emotions of leaving the Coast Guard two years ago still felt raw at times. The last thing he needed was for Kylie to feel sorry for him. "Your brother was a great rescue swimmer. I was surprised when he decided to get out of the Coast Guard."

Kylie nodded. "I guess he decided he'd had enough excitement in his life. So he came back to Kentucky and became a police officer instead."

Nate thought of what his second career choice

had been, before the restaurant had been given to him. He'd been offered a position as instructor at the Coast Guard Training Center in Yorktown. Every day, he questioned whether or not he should have taken that position there. But his father's wishes had been for him to take over this place after he died. How could he say no to the man who'd sacrificed so much for him? Besides, that last mission always seemed to haunt him.

His gaze focused on Kylie for a moment, and he could see her studying him, probably trying to figure him out. Few people had ever accomplished that task. She shifted her weight, and Nate waited to hear what she'd say next.

"I think Bruce misses the Coast Guard. I know he really loved it."

"We had some good times. That's for sure."

When he saw Kylie's earnest expression, Nate thought about telling her that he missed it also. But then he might have to tell her about that last rescue he'd attempted. About the failure that still haunted him and drove him to be the person he was today.

When Kylie got back to her room, her back ached,

her feet hurt and her head pounded. She wasn't used to being on her feet all day, bending over a chopping board for hours at a time, or trying to remember a list of new recipes. She worked hard on her local cooking show and for her catering business, but it was nothing like this.

She lay back in bed and kicked her feet up. What she wouldn't do for a TV to distract her thoughts right now. Or a good book. Well, she had a good book, but she wouldn't be reading it. Not with that reminder written in the front of it.

Instead, her mind wandered to her conversation with Bruce today. The Man in Black was getting brave, breaking into her apartment like that. He'd broken in once before to leave her a note. That hand-jotted letter had been one of the first clues that whoever followed her wasn't merely a harmless fan. After that, the pictures began coming. The photos proved that wherever she went, this man followed her.

She pulled her arms around her chest. The man had never touched her but still she'd felt so violated. She prayed he would be caught soon. Then she could get out of this tiny apartment and away from Nate Richardson.

His image—as handsome as it might be—flashed in her head and she frowned.

It wasn't that she didn't like Nate. She couldn't help but feel she was in his way, that he didn't really want her here.

She sighed. She'd done enough thinking. Thinking always got her in trouble.

She reached over to her nightstand and grabbed her cell phone. She'd laid out the pieces this morning, hoping the electronics would dry out. She snapped the battery back in and pressed the "on" button. A moment later, her screen lit up.

"Yes, it works." She didn't intend to leave the phone on during her stay here, but it was nice to have, just in case she needed to get in touch with someone in an emergency.

The phone buzzed and a message popped up on the screen informing her that she had four new voice mail messages. Probably all from Nate or Bruce last night. She anticipated hearing their anxious voices, asking her where she was and why she wasn't answering.

The first two messages, as she expected, were from Bruce and the third from Nate. She anticipated the fourth being from Bruce as well. Instead, a gravelly voice filled her ears.

"Where are you, Kylie? You think you can run from me, but you can't. I'll find you, wherever you go. Remember that. I'm always watching."

Kylie scavenged the cupboards the next morning only to discover she had no food in her little kitchenette. Her stomach rumbling with hunger, she got dressed and headed downstairs. Certainly Nate wouldn't mind if she hunted around the restaurant for something to eat.

When she found some free time, she'd buy some groceries. But if Nate worked her as hard today as he'd done yesterday, she'd never have the chance to go shopping. If what Suzy had told her was true, it was no wonder the man couldn't keep any employees around.

As she padded downstairs, she shivered, remembering the voice mail she'd listened to last night. How far away would she have to be from her life in Kentucky before she felt safe? Would she ever feel safe?

She pushed through the doors into the kitchen, and the scent of bacon and eggs drifted out. Nate stood at the griddle wearing a white apron and what was perhaps a warm smile. Could it be?

"Morning." He turned over an omelet and turned toward her.

Yep, that was the start of a small smile. It looked nice on him.

Kylie had to turn her approving gaze away from her temporary boss. She always found something very attractive about a man in the kitchen. Instead of dwelling on the image, she leaned against the counter and crossed her arms. "Smells good."

Using tongs, he picked up a piece of bacon from the griddle and placed it on a plate with an omelet. He handed the dish to her. "I thought you might be hungry and I realized I didn't leave you any food."

"This more than makes up for it." She placed the food on the counter while going to grab two ceramic mugs. "Want me to grab you a cup of coffee? You will be joining me for breakfast, won't you?"

"I usually just share the breakfast nook with a newspaper. I suppose a change in company could be good." A hint of a smile tugged at the corner of his mouth.

She poured the hot liquid into the cups and carried them to a table at the front. As she waited for Nate, she took the opportunity to soak in the dining area. Nate had created a nice atmosphere—one that fit in with his Revolutionary theme by keeping a post-and-beam design, low ceilings, chandeliers with electric candles and simple, mission-style tables and chairs. The floors were wooden and rustic-looking, and a few antiques were scattered along the walls. Now all he needed were waitresses dressed in period attire.

A moment later, Nate joined her with two steaming plates of food. A moment of awkward silence followed as they both began eating. What exactly did they have to talk about? It seemed all they had in common were her brother and cooking, the latter of which Nate apparently couldn't stand.

"Good omelet," she finally said. She told the truth. The eggs were delicious and cooked perfectly.

"Thanks. Breakfast is my meal of choice any day of the week." He took another bite and eyed her a moment. After swallowing he said, "So tell me more about your show and your catering business. You seem to enjoy cooking."

She wiped her mouth and nodded. "I do enjoy cooking. Always have. I like taking everyday, ordinary foods and making them . . . extraordinary. All it usually takes is some fresh herbs or an unexpected ingredient and—voila!—the whole dish can come alive."

"Maybe you'll show me one of those dishes sometime." She nodded again, contemplating whether or not she should offer her ideas about his restaurant. No, she decided, she wouldn't overstep her boundaries. "I've always loved food, ever since I was little. I always wanted to help my mom in the kitchen or make meals for my friends. I did go to culinary school, but only for a year. At that point, my friend and I began getting offered catering jobs— first for our friends' weddings or church functions. But business really began picking up, and we started doing a lot for some high-end clients and companies."

"How did you get your own cooking show?"

"One of my clients opened a kitchen shop—you know, one of those stores that sell every imaginable tool for the kitchen? She started asking me to come in and do demonstrations. I did, and I discovered I loved it. While I was doing a demonstration, a producer from a local network saw me. He asked me to come in and do a screen test. I really fumbled the first few times in front of the camera, but for some reason, the producer saw potential in me."

Kylie paused to take a sip of coffee.

"I tried to do both the catering business and the show for a while, but it finally got to be too much. I'm still a partner in the catering business, but I ended up going full-time with the show, which is now syndicated on a few different stations in

Kentucky. I'm by no means famous, but it does feel good to have your hard work recognized." She put down her coffee, relishing the feeling of accomplishment, followed by the disappointment caused by this derailment in her plans. "And now, here I am. What more is there to say?"

Nate nodded and wiped his mouth. "I'm sure this guy will be caught soon and you'll be able to resume your life."

If only Kylie could be that certain. She licked her lips and leaned back in her chair. "So, you've heard all about me. Tell me about this place. Your father opened it, correct?"

"Twenty years ago. This was his big dream that he saved his entire life for. Finally, he quit his job at the motor plant where he worked on the assembly line and opened this place. Spent every cent of his savings and retirement here."

"Wow. That's a great story. I always like hearing about people pursuing their dreams. Was the restaurant everything he'd hoped it would be?"

"My dad loved it. It was more than a restaurant for him. This place was like a big old kitchen table where people would come and gather around. It didn't matter if he knew you or not. As soon as you walked through the doors, you were his guest."

"That sounds wonderful." She shifted in her seat. "Do you mind if I ask what happened to your father?"

The smile disappeared from Nate's face, a grim expression replacing it. "Three years ago, he had a heart attack. The doctor diagnosed him with coronary heart disease. In five months, he deteriorated quickly. Then the second heart attack hit a year after the first one. That one killed him on the spot."

"That's terrible. I'm so sorry."

"At least I still have this place. It makes me feel close to Dad, like his spirit is still here overseeing everything."

"Where's your mom?"

"She died when I was a kid. Cancer."

Cancer. Every time Kylie heard the word, she felt a pang of sadness and grief and understanding. "You must have been an only child."

"The doctors told my parents they'd never have kids. But to their surprise, when my mom turned thirty-nine, she found out she was pregnant."

Kylie took the last bite of her omelet. "I'm sure it was the best surprise she could have ever gotten."

Nate smiled. "That's what she always said."

Silence fell again and Kylie wiped her mouth. She stood, her chair shrieking against the floor.

"That was delicious, but I guess I should get busy in the kitchen."

Nate grabbed her hand. "Wait."

Kylie ignored the jolt of electricity that rushed through her and paused, her heart racing for no good reason. "Yes?"

"Could you sit back down for a minute?"

Kylie nodded and obeyed, a sick feeling forming in her gut. Conversations like this always put her on edge, and Nate's eyes looked far too worried for her comfort. "Yes?"

"I've been thinking about you . . . about your situation, I mean." His fingers locked together on the table, like a father's might before a stern talk. "I really think it's best that, while you're here, you don't go anywhere alone. This man who's been after you is obviously unstable. I want you to feel safe here, but the reality is that until this man is behind bars, you're better to be cautious."

Indignation rushed through her. She'd fought for her entire life to get to the place she was today. She'd overcome the stereotypes that came with being petite, soft-spoken and kind. She'd risen up from the hardships she'd endured and shown she was capable and confident and savvy. The last thing she needed was someone trying to take that from her.

Kylie swallowed, choosing her words carefully. "Thank you for your concern. I realize that I need to take every precaution possible. I do. But the last thing I need is someone dictating where I go and when and with whom."

Nate's eyes flickered, though Kylie wasn't sure what the emotion was behind them. Anger? Curiosity? Admiration? "Kylie, I really think it would be in your best interest to listen to me on this one."

She bristled. She was wise enough to know she didn't need to wear a bull's-eye on her back or act like a sitting duck, so to speak. "I've been living on my own for seven years now. I think I can trust my own instincts and make my own decisions."

Nate cleared his throat and when he spoke again, his voice sounded lower. "This isn't about making your own decisions. It's about being smart and staying safe."

"I assure you that I'll use the utmost wisdom." Kylie tried to suppress her frustration. Her efforts didn't work. Her hands clenched into fists.

Nate closed his eyes, as if frustrated himself. "Kylie, I'm not trying to tell you what to do."

"It sounds like that's exactly what you're trying to

do." She took a deep breath and softened her voice. "I appreciate you letting me stay here, Nate, and I'm more than happy to help out at the restaurant to pay for room and board. But I don't need a guardian or someone telling me what to do."

"I think you're misunderstanding me—"

"Maybe this isn't the best time to talk about this." She stood and hurried into the kitchen before she said something she'd regret and began prepping for the day.

Nate watched Kylie walk away and shook his head.

The Coast Guard had taught him a lot about rescuing people. Some people were anxious for your help, and even after the mission was over they'd make it their mission to publicly thank you and tell others about what you'd done. Others were more difficult. Some people tried to pull you underwater in their panic to be saved. Still other people wanted to be rescued but were too afraid to take the necessary steps, too afraid to trust you. Sometimes you had to literally knock them out in order to save their lives.

Kylie was obviously going to fall into the "difficult to rescue" category. She wanted help, but she wanted to save herself at the same time. She'd been forced to trust him but wasn't sure how far to take that trust. Nate could understand that. But he also knew that the most important thing was keeping her safe, whether she wanted his help or not.

He sighed, ready for the challenge but not the drama that might come with it.

He gathered the plates on the table and bused them into the kitchen. Kylie stood with her back toward him, chopping carrots and onions. By the force of her chopping, she made a clear statement that she did not want to be bothered. Nate was fine with that. If he spoke to Kylie now, the words that left his mouth might not be kind.

He went about his tasks to prepare for opening. The crowds were always bigger on Saturdays than weekdays, so they prepared for more. By ten o'clock, the rest of the staff wandered in, looking less than thrilled to be working today. The sun did shine bright outside this morning and the weatherman had promised some of the nicest weather they'd had since last fall. Most people didn't want to spend days like today inside.

At noon, customers began coming in, most of them tourists visiting for the day. Being busy probably benefited both Nate and Kylie because, in the rush of things, chances for more unpleasant exchanges were limited.

He noticed Kylie seemed to warm up toward the rest of the staff while completely avoiding him. She was efficient in the kitchen though, so he couldn't complain. He wished he could hire someone with her work ethic permanently. When would Kylie be leaving? Possibly in just a couple of days.

When they finally had a lull in customers, Nate excused himself and went upstairs to his apartment. He picked up his cell phone and dialed Bruce's number. He'd been thinking about everything that Kylie had told him and now he wanted the inside scoop from his friend.

Bruce answered on the first ring, his voice tight, worried.

Nate assured him everything was okay. "I want to ask you about this man who's been following Kylie. She told me he broke into her house yesterday."

"We searched for clues as to this guy's identity, but we haven't found anything yet. Whoever he is, he's good. Leaves no detail unnoticed. He's been like that since the beginning."

Nate narrowed his eyes. "Everyone screws up sometimes. Everyone."

"That's what we're counting on."

Nate shifted his weight, looking out his window at three cars that pulled in front of the restaurant. They'd need his help downstairs soon, but right now he had to get more information. "Any update on the sting?"

"It's scheduled for Friday. We want to make sure we do this right, with no mistakes." Bruce's voice held no room for question. "I'm afraid that if this guy ever sees Kylie again, her life will be on the line. This isn't someone who's just playing a game anymore. This guy is obsessed."

Nate bristled at his friend's words, at once glad that Kylie was here. "You think this guy knows where she went?"

"We're telling people she's on a road trip, trying to get some more inspiration and do some research for her cooking show. I won't feel safe until this guy is behind bars. He always seems to be one step ahead of us."

One step ahead of them. Maybe this guy was someone who knew Kylie personally or who could eavesdrop on her at work. "There was nothing in her apartment that would indicate where she'd gone, right? Do we need to find somewhere else for her to stay?"

"No, we don't think so. She said the only place she wrote your address down was on her notebook, but she tore that sheet off and brought it with her. We think she's safe. Believe me, the moment I start thinking she's in danger again, you'll be one of the first people who knows." Bruce paused a moment. "How's it going so far? Is she holding up okay?"

Nate contemplated his answer. "She's jumpy, which is to be expected. But she's been a big help in the kitchen. When I suggested, however, that she go nowhere alone, she got a bit miffed at me."

"She doesn't like people fussing over her. But she doesn't have much choice in this situation. Besides, she'll get over it. She always does."

"Good to know. Thanks, Bruce."

"Call me anytime, especially if anything suspicious happens. In the meantime, I'll keep you updated on what's happening here. I hope to end this nightmare once and for all."

"For Kylie's sake, I hope you do, too."

He hung up the phone and tried not to think about the possibility that Kylie's stalker had any clue she was here in Yorktown. But Bruce's words rang in his head. *He always seems to be one step ahead of us.*

Nate prayed he wasn't one step ahead of them this time.

7

*K*ylie scrubbed the inside of the refrigerator with enough tenacity to even make a military man proud.

Anything beat talking to Nate at this point, and since the dining room was empty and the fridge needed to be cleaned, she decided to stay busy rather than risk a conversation. He was proving himself to be bossy and overprotective, two qualities that she abhorred.

Yet why did she seem drawn to those very types? She scrubbed even harder. Her ex-boyfriend had been the alpha male type. But the strength she'd originally been attracted to she'd eventually begun to despise. Colin liked to assert himself, tell her what to do, even what to wear and who to hang out with.

Thankfully, she'd realized the wrong path that relationship was taking early enough to get out. She'd never put herself in that position again. She scrubbed harder as she thought about it. Why had she allowed herself to be treated like that?

She threw the scrub brush back into a bucket, satisfied that there wasn't a crumb out of place, and glanced at the clock. Closing time. Without a word to Nate, she climbed the stairs to her apartment.

Kylie took a long shower to get the smell of grease out of her hair. Then she put on some comfy sweats and a sweatshirt and plopped in a mustard-yellow swivel chair, the most comfortable thing she could find in the apartment, other than her bed.

She stared at the empty apartment. No sofa, no TV, no radio. What was she going to do with herself? And tomorrow was Sunday. Nate had informed her that the restaurant was closed on Sundays, which meant she had an entire day to do nothing.

She'd overheard customers today talking about how nice the weather was supposed to be all weekend. Perhaps she could explore Yorktown a little bit, get some fresh air.

She twirled around in the chair as Nate's admonishment played in her head. No, going out alone wouldn't be wise. Perhaps one of the waitresses, either Carrie or Suzy, was available? Probably not. They were in their early twenties and seemed more like the type to go clubbing than show a twenty-nine-year-old around an historical area.

Kylie sighed and sank deeper into the stiff chair. She pictured what she might be doing if she were at home right now. She'd probably be at a movie with her best friend, Dina. If not, it would only be because her producer, Larry, had pestered her into working overtime to come up with some new recipes for the show.

She had to credit much of the success of the show to Larry, though his overly ambitious ways drove her crazy most of the time. Both Larry and Dina had known about her stalker and tried to keep her safe—and occupied, which Kylie appreciated.

A knock at the door put Kylie on edge. She glanced at her watch. Eleven-thirty? Who would be knocking on her door at this hour? Only Nate had a key to unlock the restaurant door, but still, intruders could be clever, silent on the prowl.

Kylie grabbed the only weapon she could find—a lamp—and crept toward the door. The knock came again, more quickly this time. She licked her lips, trying to find her words.

"Kylie, it's me, Nate. Open up." He paused. "Please."

Nate? She let out the breath she held and jerked the door open, scowling as she did so. "Yes?"

His gaze wandered to her hand. "I didn't mean to scare you."

"I'm just being cautious." She put the lamp on the table and turned back to him. "Do you need something?"

He jammed his hands into his jean pockets. "I thought you might need a ride to church tomorrow."

"That's nice of you, but I don't go to church. I haven't been in years."

His face registered surprise. "Oh, I just assumed . . ."

Kylie shrugged. "It's okay. I appreciate the offer."

He shifted his weight from one foot to the other. "Do you need anything?"

"A time machine, so I can fast-forward until after this man is caught and I can finally live again."

Nate frowned and shook his head. "I'd give you one if I had it. But since I don't, you're stuck with me for a while."

Kylie frowned also. "Stuck with him" was just the phrase she'd use.

Nate was surprised when he walked downstairs Sunday morning and saw Kylie waiting at the back door, looking lovely in crisp slacks and a flowing white blouse. Her long dark hair had been pulled back in a clip and small earrings dangled from her ears.

"Morning," he muttered when he reached her by the door. Her gaze only fluttered to his. "Morning. I changed my mind about church. I hope that's okay."

"Of course it is. I'm glad you're coming." Truth was, he'd been utterly surprised by her flat rejection last night. He couldn't put his finger on it, but Kylie just seemed like the kind of girl who went to church. Hearing that she didn't really threw him for a loop.

"I was hoping we might stop at the store afterward, if that's okay. I need to pick up a few things."

"No problem."

He unlocked the door and extended his arm outside. "Ladies first."

As she stepped outside, Nate caught a whiff of her perfume, which smelled like sweet flowers on a spring day. He caught himself wanting to stand there and absorb the scent for a little longer.

Instead, he locked up the building and directed

Kylie to his truck, a well-used model that just begged for a construction project so it could haul stuff around. He opened the passenger-side door for Kylie, catching the scent of her perfume again as she slid inside.

A few minutes later they were rumbling down the road. Kylie sat beside him with her hands folded in her lap, her gaze focused out the window.

"Sleep okay?" He tried to start up at least a semblance of a conversation.

"I haven't slept well in six months." Her eyes remained fixed outside. Finally, her head swiveled toward him. "That may be the reason I've been a little testy lately. Sorry if I've bitten your head off. I don't quite feel like myself."

"Stress can do that to a person."

"I know, but it's still no excuse for treating someone poorly." She rubbed her fingers together in her lap, as if in deep thought.

"Apology accepted, then. I'm not always the most pleasant person to be around at the restaurant either, so I probably don't deserve that apology." He drummed his fingers on the steering wheel as he pulled to a stop at a deserted intersection.

Kylie drew in a deep breath and slowly exhaled. "So, tell me about your church."

"You'll love it. It's smallish, but the people are great. We just got a new pastor a few months ago and he can preach a great sermon."

"I look forward to it then."

He ventured forward with the question that had been on his mind since last night. "So you really don't go to church back in Lexington?"

She shook her head. "Not very often. I always tell myself I should get back in the habit, yet I never seem to do it. No good reason. I guess I've just gotten lazy . . . or maybe lukewarm."

"It's easy to let that happen."

She raised a brow and sighed. "It sure is. Too easy."

He wanted to ask her more but didn't. She'd share more about her spiritual walk if she wanted to. The rest of the trip was silent until he finally pulled up to the steepled brick building where he'd been attending church for the last twenty years.

"Cute," Kylie mumbled as she climbed out. "Reminds me of a postcard."

Inside, Nate introduced Kylie to several people, explaining that she was trying to get some restaurant experience. He didn't want anyone else to know the real reason she was here. The last thing he needed was people asking questions or going digging for more information.

Though Kylie said she hadn't been to church in a while, she seemed comfortable and sang along with the songs with hardly a glance at the hymnal. Her hostility seemed to be gone, and for a little while, she even seemed halfway relaxed.

Darlene and Harvey caught them after the service was over and gave them both a big hug. Kylie's face lit up when she spotted them.

"What are you two doing for lunch?" Darlene asked, still holding on to Kylie at arm's length.

"No plans." Nate stole a glance at Kylie.

"Come with us to get some barbecue. She's got to have some of Hank's while she's here," Darlene said. "It's the best. The vinegar-based sauce just makes your mouth tingle before crying out for more."

Kylie nodded at him, her eyes brighter than they'd been all day. "Sounds good to me. I'm always up for some local cuisine."

"Let's go then." Nate extended his arm toward the church door.

In his truck, Kylie pulled out her cell phone and the digital chimes indicated she'd turned it on. A moment later, her face went white.

"Everything okay?" Nate asked.

She turned her big eyes on him and Nate saw fear in their depths. "Would you do me a favor?"

"Sure thing."

"Will you listen to my messages and tell me if there's anything important?"

He left his truck in Park. "Your voice mail messages?"

She nodded. "There are ten. If it's the man who's been stalking me, I don't think I can bear to hear his voice and I'm nearly certain these messages are from him."

He took the phone from her and pressed the OK button. A raspy voice came on the line. "You can run but you can't hide, Kylie. Do you think I won't find you?" A diabolical laugh followed.

The next message was much of the same. "No one can hide from me, especially not you, Kylie Summers. The world is small and getting smaller by the moment."

Each of the messages featured the same gravelly voice. With each new voice mail message, the man sounded increasingly unstable. Nate could hear the anger rising in the pitch of the man's voice, in the clipped syllables, in the emotion behind the words. The last message summed up his threat. "I will find you, Kylie.

And when I do, you'll be sorry you ever ran away."

Kylie watched Nate with wide eyes. Her hands trembled in her lap. "It's not good. I can see it on your face." Her voice sounded subdued, like she'd accepted the nightmare her life had become.

He closed her phone, careful to save all the messages in case the police needed them as evidence once this guy was caught. Then he turned his gaze on Kylie, taking a deep breath as he carefully measured his words. "I'm glad you're here, Kylie. This guy's losing it. He's cracking."

Kylie looked far off, like she was in some other place, some other time. Then she turned to Nate, her face expressionless. "What if he tracks me here?"

"How would he do that?"

She threw her hands in the air. "How did he do anything else that he's done? He managed to break into my apartment without leaving a bit of trace evidence behind. He seems to know where I'll be before I get there. He even knows how to terrorize me when I'm six hundred miles away."

Nate's heart plunged. He had the urge to grab her hand, to try and offer her some comfort. But he didn't. They barely knew each other. "Your brother is a good police officer. If he has even an inkling that you're in trouble here, he'll move you again."

Kylie's face crumbled when he said, "He'll move you again."

"You okay?" he asked.

"I'm just tired of my life feeling like it's in an upheaval. I want this guy arrested and behind bars and out of my life. I want things to be normal again."

"You do realize that even when this guy is caught, it's still going to be a process, right? There will be a trial. He'll hopefully be sentenced and be locked up for a long, long time. But that's not always the case."

She drew in a deep breath, her gaze again focusing on something out the window. "Yeah, I do realize that. I just keep hoping for the best-case scenario. One person shouldn't be allowed this much control in my life."

He put the truck into drive and pulled onto the highway. "What would you be doing on a normal Sunday back in Kentucky, Kylie?"

She looked into the distance and the vague hint of a smile curled one side of her mouth. "I would have probably slept in. My producer, Larry, would probably call me, wanting me to work overtime. I would refuse, claiming I need—and deserve—at least one day of rest per week. Then I'd probably go out with my friend Dina to lunch and we'd spend the day chatting or shopping."

"It sounds like your producer is pretty pushy."

She shrugged. "He wants to take the show to 'the next level.'" She rolled her eyes as her hands made air quotes around the last three words, indicating she'd heard them a million times before. "We have someone interested in taking the show national, and that's been all Larry has talked about."

"What is your goal?"

"To cook." She turned a sheepish smile toward him. "I just love cooking and sharing what I've prepared with other people. It's like sharing a piece of my heart with them."

Nate smiled and rubbed his chin, still smooth from the morning's shave. "You would have liked my dad. You sound like him."

"There's just something about coming around the table with other people and sharing food and conversation that makes everything balance out. All of your other worries go away, for at least an hour or two."

"You have a nice way of describing eating."

Kylie smiled. "Most men just think of eating in terms of food, of satisfying a grumbling stomach.

There's so much more to it, though. Food can be a way to show people how much you care for them."

Some strange emotion panged in his gut. He had the brief thought of having someone to take care of him, someone to delight in preparing his favorite meals and longing to hear about his day when he got home from work. Instead, he cooked meals for other people and went home to an empty apartment just in time to fall in bed every night. The thought weighed on him, but he shoved down the emotion.

They pulled to a stop in front of a small restaurant nestled in the woods with a country road the only path leading there. The place itself looked like an old house that had been converted into a restaurant. But the appearance of Hank's did nothing to affect its business. People came from miles around to eat the barbecue here.

If only he could say the same about his restaurant.

"It's not much to look at, but the food is good." Nate saw the doubt on her face.

Harvey and Darlene waited on the porch, waving at them. Nate tried to put the voice mail messages out of his mind as they joined them by the front door. But the stalker's voice wouldn't leave his mind. He could only imagine what it was doing to Kylie.

If that man found her here in Yorktown, there was no telling how he'd lash out. From what Nate understood, the man had never been violent with Kylie before. Nate would bet by the sound of those messages and the threats he'd given that the man would want to make sure Kylie never went off his radar again.

"Nate?"

He snapped away from his thoughts and saw Kylie staring at him, her eyebrows scrunched together in concern. She nodded toward the dining room. "They're waiting to seat us."

He took her elbow and directed her behind Harvey and Darlene. "Let's not keep them waiting, then."

Despite the fact that he tried to appear nonchalant, he'd be keeping a closer eye on Kylie, making sure there was no one suspicious watching her from the shadows. Not on his watch.

8

Kylie enjoyed the pulled-pork barbecue, served on a bun with chunky coleslaw and lots of tangy hot sauce. Even the french fries, hand-cut and cooked in peanut oil, exceeded her expectations with a nice crunchy outside and warm moist inside.

But even better than the food was the conversation. Harvey and Darlene kept her entertained with their banter and their good-natured ribbing of Nate. Nate took it well, smiling and laughing pleasantly. Maybe Kylie had misjudged Nate. When he stepped away from his restaurant, he actually seemed likable.

"Ready to go?" Nate looked at her from across the table.

Kylie nodded. "I am. The food was wonderful. I'm really glad you brought me here."

"You're going to take her to see Colonial Williamsburg and Jamestown while she's here, aren't you?" Darlene gave Nate a pointed look. "And, of course, she's got to get a guided tour of Yorktown, the place where the Revolutionary War was won. It's only the best little town in America. That's my unbiased opinion."

Kylie could see Nate trying to come up with an excuse as to why he couldn't be her tour guide. She put him out of his misery. "I'm sure I won't have time. I won't be in town long, and while I'm here I want to get all the experience I can at Nate's restaurant."

"How's it going so far? Nate's not working you too hard, is he?" Harvey leaned across the table on his elbows and suspended his shaggy eyebrows. "If he is, I'm going to have to have a little talk with him." His raised his eyebrows higher in exaggerated anger.

Kylie laughed. "No, he's not. Besides, hard work is good for the soul."

Darlene winked at Nate. "I knew I liked this girl for some reason. She's pretty *and* she likes to work hard. Now that's a great combination."

They all chuckled as they stood and went outside

to their cars. The sun felt warm on Kylie's shoulders, even though the breeze had a slight chill to it.

After Kylie had climbed into Nate's truck, he turned to her. "Where to? Grocery store? Mall? Drugstore?"

"The grocery store is fine. I just need to pick up a few things to hold me over until I go back home."

Nate went inside the grocery store with her, and Kylie didn't miss how he scanned every aisle. Bruce had said she'd be safe with Nate, and apparently he was right. Nate never seemed to let down his guard.

After Kylie paid for her groceries, they went back to the truck and started to Yorktown. Silence stretched between them as the truck rumbled down the road.

Ten minutes into the trip, Nate finally spoke. "Listen, I was thinking that this might be your only opportunity while you're here to see the town. What do you say we put these groceries away and go explore Yorktown? It's nice outside. You never know around here. It could be snowing tomorrow."

Kylie wondered about his sudden change in plans. Earlier he'd seemed dead-set against showing her around town. What had changed his mind? "A tour of Yorktown sounds nice. But I don't want impose on you."

"It would be my pleasure."

Were his words sincere? For the time being, she'd believe they were. Besides, spending the afternoon with Nate beat being cooped up in that apartment until the morning.

After putting the groceries away, Kylie changed into jeans, a sweater and some tennis shoes. Nate promptly knocked on her door at the promised time. When Kylie saw him, she again had to suck in a breath. Even dressed in jeans and a casual, button-down shirt he made her heart race inexplicably.

The last thing she needed from her visit here in Yorktown was to develop a crush on someone who already considered her a burden.

She stepped out of her apartment, looking away from Nate in hopes of slowing her heart down.

"You mind walking?" Nate asked as they walked down the stairs.

"Some exercise would be nice."

She stuffed her hands into the pockets of her sweatshirt as they started toward the sandy beach across from the restaurant. As they walked, seagulls cried their sad songs as they circled overhead, looking for bread crumbs or any other food that the sparse crowd on the beach might offer. The sand cushioned Kylie's feet and gentle waves lapped at the shore. A group of college kids played Frisbee in the distance and a young family picnicked on a blanket.

Kylie noticed that despite the difference in their heights, her and Nate's strides matched well. Colin had always been a fast walker, and she'd had to practically race to keep up with him. He'd had a brisk pace, while she enjoyed taking life at a more leisurely speed. She liked the fact that Nate walked with his hands casually stuffed into his jeans, looking as if he enjoyed simply being around the water.

After walking around a rock jetty, Nate showed her a historic cave that nestled into the bluff. Cornwallis's Cave, he'd said. Then they started down the pier that jutted out into the river. Several people fished off the side of the wooden structure, while others took pictures or simply looked at the beautiful river in front of them. Nate and Kylie walked to the end and leaned against the railing. Out in the river, three rubber-sided rescue boats skimmed the water.

Nate pointed to them. "Those are Coast Guard boats. They're doing training exercises. The Training

Center isn't too far from here, so you'll see a lot of these exercises while you're here."

"Bruce said you received a medal of honor before you retired from the Coast Guard. He always spoke —speaks, I should say—highly of you." Kylie watched Nate as his eyes focused on the crews out in the water. "Do you miss the Coast Guard?"

"It was my life, what I'd always wanted to do since I was a boy. I would come out here and watch practice exercises similar to these on the river. I knew that's what I wanted. In high school, I took swim lessons and worked the summers as a lifeguard in Virginia Beach. Whatever I could do to get experience. After high school, I enlisted and went through training in Elizabeth City, North Carolina. I spent the rest of my career there as an aviation survival technician, also known as a helicopter rescue swimmer."

"Why did you get out when you did, then?" Kylie inhaled deeply as the scent of river water blew up with the breeze.

He shrugged. "So I could take over the restaurant. You know what they say about the best-laid plans..."

"I do. I really thought I wanted to play oboe for the symphony one day."

"What happened?"

She sucked in a breath. "In high school, I got accepted into a national music program, one that would look great on my resume. I thought my life was laid out in front of me."

"Your dad was a music teacher, right?"

Kylie nodded. "Yes, and he was thrilled that I wanted to follow in his footsteps and pursue music. I think he'd always wanted to play music for a living instead of teach, but life didn't work out that way for him."

"I have a feeling there's a 'but' in here somewhere for you, too." Nate glanced at her, his eyes showing he had truly taken an interest in the conversation.

Kylie licked her lips, leaning still against the railing of the pier as she vividly remembered that time of her life. "A week before I was supposed to leave for the music program, I was diagnosed with lymphoma."

Nate's eyes widened. "Cancer?"

She nodded. "Yep. Cancer. At sixteen. It's not a diagnosis you expect to hear."

"I can't imagine." His voice sounded soft, as if he really cared. "What happened?"

That period of her life came back in a flash of

vivid memories. "I decided not to go to the program.
I had more important things to do, things like
chemo. The cancer took a year to beat. But I did." At
just the mention of chemo, the scar from her
medical port began to throb. It also reminded her of
the obstacles she'd overcome in life.

"How did this lead to you becoming a chef?"

"I thought playing the oboe would help me
through the tough days. But it didn't. Cooking did.
Whenever I wasn't nauseous from treatments or
medications, I cooked. Being in the kitchen helped
me keep my sanity. That's when I knew what I
wanted to do."

She was already the youngest of four siblings in
the family, prone to being babied. But when the
lymphoma diagnosis had come, everyone had
stepped it up to another level. Suddenly she was
fragile, and somehow that translated into being
incompetent to make her own decisions, as well.

Her fight for independence had begun then.
Her parents didn't hover over her as much
anymore—they'd retired to Florida. Her other
siblings had also moved to various parts of the
country, but Bruce still lived close and worried
about her enough to make up for everyone else's
absence.

"How have you been doing since the chemo ended?"

"I've been cancer-free for twelve years."

"Praise God."

Kylie wished she could agree with him, but the scars from the disease had lasted longer than she'd anticipated. Praising God was the last thing she'd been doing since her diagnosis. A disease that had once pulled her closer to her Creator now pulled them apart.

Once in remission, she'd begun to ask herself why—why had God chosen her to go through that whole ordeal? What had she done to deserve that punishment? She'd allowed those questions to cause a rift between her and God.

She'd assumed the gap would close with time, that the questions would fade. Instead, she'd stepped further away from God. She'd never felt as far away as she did now.

Nate vaguely remembered Bruce telling him about his sister's illness. By the time he and Bruce had met, Kylie must have been in remission. Now that he thought about it, for as long as Nate had known

Bruce, Bruce had been worried about his sister for one reason or another. Now he knew why.

He stole another glance at Kylie, wishing he had some uninterrupted time to soak in her delicate profile. No wonder she was so stubborn. If she could beat cancer, she probably thought she could beat anything.

They watched the Coast Guard crew perform a few more exercises before walking back to the beach and continuing down the shore. Nate felt sure Kylie's stalker wasn't here, but still he scanned the people out enjoying the day. He'd learned in the Coast Guard that you always had to be aware of your surroundings so you could search out any potential threats. He never would have thought he'd be using that training now to protect Kylie.

As they neared the shopping area of town, the sound of Yorktown's Fife and Drum filled the air, the melody patriotic and eerie at the same time. Kylie paused and put her hand on Nate's arm. He ignored the jolt that electrified him at her touch.

She closed her eyes as if delighting in the moment. "That sound is just magical. It makes me feel . . ."

"Like you've been transported back in time?"

"Exactly. It's fabulous."

Nate smiled. A group of tourists approached them on a walking tour while a guide dressed in period attire told them stories of the town.

"That's actually the ghost tour," Nate whispered. "All of the buildings in this area are old and almost all of them have some sort of ghost story. Tourists eat it up."

Kylie's gaze scanned the crowd. "That's a lot of tourists. I bet it's tempting to keep the restaurant open today."

"It is. I bet we'd do great business. But that was one of my father's wishes for the restaurant, that it be closed on Sundays so we could honor the Lord's Day. I had to respect his wishes."

"That's admirable. And wise, really, especially since you work so much already. You need one day of rest. It's good for the soul."

Somehow, Kylie's words brought an unusual comfort to him. Everyone seemed to think the decision was ill-advised, especially since the restaurant was struggling. Hearing Kylie agree with his choice gave him a sense of affirmation and comfort.

Kylie continued to stroll, her hands stuffed deep into her pockets. She looked casual and comfortable as the breeze blew her hair away from her face and revealed her creamy skin. For some reason, when

Bruce had asked him about Kylie coming here, he'd continually pictured a little girl, a "little sister" being here under his care. Kylie was anything but a girl.

"You asked me how I usually spend my Sundays." Kylie glanced over at him. "What do you usually do on your day of rest?"

"Church, lunch." Nate paused, realizing he was about to incriminate himself. "Then I usually do paperwork for the restaurant. You know—place orders to the distributors, make up the work schedule, etc."

"I guess I can't say anything. Sure, I take Sundays off, but I haven't had a vacation in months. Longer than months. It's probably been more than a year, truth be told." She kicked a rock. "Of course, everyone thinks I'm on vacation right now." She threw her hands up and laughed. "Yes, this is my vacation. My life sounds a little pathetic, doesn't it?"

Nate didn't think Kylie sounded pathetic at all. She sounded like a hard worker, doing what she could to make it. Wasn't that the American dream? To pursue your passions, to work hard, to get ahead?

They walked in silence down the historic streets, Nate enjoying the day more than he would have thought he would. Kylie made for decent company. When the wind blew, it carried the sweet scent of

Kylie's perfume, which for some reason made his heart race. His attraction to Kylie couldn't grow any more than his initial feelings. Soon, she'd be back in Kentucky. Besides, Nate didn't have time to date and run a restaurant. Combining the two would only spell disaster.

"Do you mind if we go in here?" Kylie pointed to a gift store.

Playing tourist in his hometown had its appeal. "Of course."

The store's owner, one of the regulars at Nate's place, called a greeting before continuing to count receipts on the counter. Nate watched as Kylie delighted in all the little knickknacks featured in the store. Seeing Kylie marvel at everything in the town made his heart warm. Yorktown meant everything to him, and being with someone who appreciated the town as much as he did created a bond.

Finally, after wandering down each row of gifts, Kylie picked up a hand-thrown coffee mug with a picture of Yorktown painted on the front.

"I have to buy this." She held it up with a grin. "Then every time I look at it, I'll be reminded of how grateful I am that you gave me a place to stay."

Nate's heart panged at the proclamation. Just yesterday he'd been counting down the hours until she left. Now, for some reason, the thought of her leaving made him feel heavy.

He felt that way only because Kylie was an efficient cook, he told himself. And she required no pay for her work. Those were the things he'd miss. Not Kylie herself.

He had to admit that the day had been pleasant, though. Aside from her not-too-subtle questions about his experience in running a restaurant, he'd enjoyed her company. Her warm disposition had been a nice distraction from the obligations in his life.

"Ready?" Kylie appeared with a paper bag in hand.

"Let's go."

When they stepped outside, a familiar face in the distance caught Nate's eye. The man, clad in mostly rags and an old military jacket, emerged from between two historic houses. He paused, his back hunched, and stared at them. Nate pulled Kylie closer to him.

She looked up at him with those wide, mesmerizing eyes. "What's wrong?"

"Nothing." He nodded in the distance. "That's Frank Watters. He's the town bum, for lack of a better term. He's generally harmless, but he can get a bit aggressive sometimes."

Nate waved to him as they passed. Frank waved back, his gaze lingering on Kylie just a few minutes too long for Nate's comfort, though. The last thing Nate wanted was for Kylie to leave one danger behind in Kentucky, only to find another here.

---

9

*M*onday and Tuesday passed quickly. Two large tour groups came in for lunch, which kept both Kylie and Nate busy in the kitchen. By the time Kylie got back to her apartment each night, she showered to get the smell of grease off and then fell into bed exhausted.

By Wednesday morning, despite her busyness, the fact that the sting was scheduled to happen Friday lingered in her mind and caused her heart to race. Would the setup work? What if it didn't, what if her stalker knew she wasn't the one doing the demonstration? What would Kylie do if this plan failed?

She'd have to cross that bridge when she got there, she supposed. For now, she'd simply pray that everything went as planned and that the madman who'd made her life miserable would be caught and thrown in jail.

She checked herself in the mirror again, tucking a stray hair behind her ear, and then headed downstairs to begin another day. When she walked into the kitchen, chaos greeted her. Nate ran around, chopping vegetables one minute while talking frantically on the phone and running to the freezer to retrieve food the next.

Kylie braced herself for whatever news he would share. When he finally slammed the phone onto the counter, he turned to her with weary eyes. She wanted to touch his arm, try to calm him down. But she would be overstepping her boundaries if she did that. Instead, she kept her distance, crossing her arms over her chest.

"What's going on?"

He sighed and shook his head. "Carrie called in sick. Says she has the flu. I've been trying to call Suzy, but she's not answering her phone—probably on purpose because my number is coming up on her caller ID. Melanie and Caitlyn both have classes all day today. Without any waitresses, we might as well close."

Kylie's mind raced as she quickly tried to troubleshoot. "Why don't you get Harvey to come over and help? I bet he'd jump at the chance to have something to do."

Nate's eyebrows shot up in disbelief. "Harvey? I cannot imagine Harvey as a waiter. That would be a disaster."

"Not necessarily. He's good with people. He eats here all the time, so he knows the menu. We could help him with the rest." Nate wasn't giving Harvey nearly enough credit.

Nate shook his head. "It's a terrible idea."

Kylie shrugged, pushing away the irritation that rose when Nate quickly dismissed her suggestion. "We'll have to manage with just the two of us then. That or go with your idea and shut down for the day. What's it going to be?"

He remained silent and thought for a moment. "Wednesday's a slow day. We could do it, just you and me. Don't you think?"

"We could do it. It doesn't mean it will be a success, but we can give it our best shot."

His face turned stony. "I know you don't approve of the way I operate, Kylie, but this is the way things are going to be. We're going to be the staff today and see how it goes."

Kylie bit back the smart remark at the tip of her

tongue. "I suggest you make up a new menu for the day then, something simpler. You might even want to think about doing that permanently, for that matter."

He scowled again. "That's what people love about this place—the selection. But I agree that a smaller menu today is a good idea. You get the kitchen prepped while I go type up a new menu. We open in an hour." The next second, he disappeared into his office.

Kylie sighed and began preparing vegetables for salads and soups. Catering could be stressful enough, but working short-staffed at a restaurant would be a nightmare. Still, Nate ran the restaurant like he'd probably run his crew while in the Coast Guard.

He acted like keeping his father's wish alive was a life-or-death situation. Even worse, Kylie feared if they both survived today that maybe Nate would consider making his staff even smaller in order to cut back on payroll costs.

Honestly, Nate seemed like two different people. One Nate ran The Revolutionary Grill, got stressed and looked like he carried the burden of the world. The other Nate she'd experienced on Sunday. He was laid back, relaxed and capable of carrying on a decent conversation.

She shook her head and continued working when she heard a rap at the back door. It was Darlene, her arms full of pies and cakes. As soon as Kylie opened the door, the heavenly scents of cinnamon, sugar, chocolate and cream drifted up to her.

"Thanks, Darlene." Kylie took a couple of pies from her as Darlene stepped inside.

She looked around the quiet kitchen. "Where is everyone?"

"We're short-staffed, to say the least. We're doing an abbreviated menu today." Kylie held up the desserts. "Too bad we can't just do desserts."

Darlene leaned closer and lowered her voice. "Can't you talk some sense into Nate? You can't run a restaurant with two people. Anyone knows that."

"I've tried. It hasn't worked, though."

The sounds of the first customers rolling in alerted Kylie. She quickly told Darlene thanks before scurrying to work.

Thankfully, the improvised lunch menu was easy and required short prep times. Nate acted as waiter and brought back orders, putting on a forced smile as he served customers.

At two, a lull allowed Kylie a moment to breathe. She and Nate both grabbed a quick bite to eat in the back, listening for the bell at the door to signal someone had come in. Her whining, aching feet quieted down for a moment as she sat down with her salad.

"It's not too bad with just the two of us here, is it?" Nate took a bite of his tuna salad sandwich.

Kylie wiped her lips. "It's not ideal, but we're making it through."

"I'm glad you're here, Kylie. I don't know what I would do if you weren't."

The sincerity in his voice surprised her. Finally, she nodded in acknowledgment. "Glad I can be here."

The bell jangled. Nate started to stand, but Kylie motioned for him to stay put. "Let me."

She wiped her mouth again, stood and started toward the front, grabbing some menus on her way. Two men, both dressed in business attire, stood at the entrance. She plastered on a friendly smile as she approached them.

"Welcome to The Revolutionary Grill. Will there just be two of you?"

An older man with silver hair nodded. "Yes, ma'am," he said with a British accent. His gaze remained on her for a moment longer than Kylie expected. She pushed down her nerves, blaming them on paranoia, and led the men to a table by the window.

After handing them menus, she explained the specials. The man's gaze still remained on her, almost as if he were studying her.

Kylie's heart sped. Was this man her stalker? She wiped her palms, suddenly sweaty, against her jeans.

"Can I start you with something to drink?" Her mouth felt dry as she mumbled the words, and she noticed her hand shaking as her pen poised on the order pad.

"Just water, please," the staring man said. His companion, a younger man—maybe an assistant—said the same.

Kylie nodded and hurried back into the kitchen. Nate was cleaning up their lunch, a satisfied grin on his face. The grin disappeared when he looked up.

"Are you okay?"

She nodded and grabbed two glasses. Her hands trembled as she poured water into the glasses. "I'm fine."

Nate approached her and his hands covered hers. She stopped pouring and looked up at him. "You're not fine. What's wrong?"

She offered a half-hearted laugh, one that wasn't

quite believable even to her own ears. "I'm just being paranoid. One of the customers out there . . . it's just the way he keeps looking at me." She shook her head. "I'm probably reading too much into things."

He took the water from her hands and with a steady gaze said, "Let me serve these."

Kylie didn't argue as he hurried into the dining room. She leaned with her palms against the counter, trying to catch her breath.

Was this it? Had her stalker found her again?

Nate forced a tight smile as he approached the two men seated by the window. He placed their water on the table, trying to appear casual as he scoped them out. "Two waters. Do you gentlemen need more time to look at the menu, or are you ready to order?"

"Anything you'd recommend?" The older man leaned back in the booth, his arm draped against the back of the bench. Nate noted his crisp suit and expensive watch.

Nate shifted his weight. "The crab soup is always popular."

The man fixed his gaze on Nate. "Is The Revolutionary Grill your restaurant?"

"It is."

His gaze drifted around the dining area. "I like the Colonial theme."

"My dad opened the place. I took over for him after he died."

The man straightened, brushing off the cuffs of his dress shirt. Then he narrowed his eyes and leaned toward Nate. "Do you mind if I ask the name of the waitress who was just out here?"

Nate's muscles tensed. "I'm not sure that's a good idea. Why are you asking?"

The man seemed to sense Nate's apprehension and let out a quick laugh, raising a hand as if urging Nate to slow down his rushing thoughts. "I'm sorry. I realize how I must have come across. It's just that she looks like someone who hosts a cooking show I'm interested in."

Nate forced himself to remain calm. "Why would you be interested in a cooking show?"

The man laughed again and shook his head, looking at his companion as if the moment were hilarious. "I'm really botching this." The man stood and extended his hand. "I'm Arnold Stephens, one of the producers on Cuisine TV. We've been pursuing a small cooking show in Kentucky called *Kylie's Kitchen,* trying to convince them to take the show national on our network. Your waitress looks just like the host from the show. Forgive me for the way I came across."

Nate relaxed some, but still wasn't convinced about the sincerity of this man. The best criminals seemed trustworthy and had clever excuses for their actions. Nate wouldn't acknowledge that the man's hunch was correct. Instead, he poised with his pen on the order pad.

"Sounds like you have an interesting job. I'll have to pass that message on to my waitress. I'm sure she'll be thrilled to look like someone famous." Nate cleared his throat and raised his notepad. "Can I take your order?"

Arnold snapped his menu shut and handed it to Nate. "I think I will try the crab soup."

His friend said he would have the same.

Back in the kitchen, Kylie still leaned against the counter, looking like she'd seen a ghost. Her skin was white, her hands trembled, her breathing shallow. Her eyes fixated on Nate, waiting for his impression.

He leaned on the counter across from her. "He says he's from Cuisine TV."

"Cuisine TV?"

"Yeah. Arnold someone? Says he's been trying to talk you into going national with your show."

Kylie's shoulders slumped and her head dropped back as she looked at the ceiling in what appeared to be relief . . . or was it disbelief? "Arnold Stephens?"

"You've heard of him?" Nate finally asked.

Kylie nodded and rubbed the space between her eyes. "My producer at our local network has been talking to him for the past few months. Mr. Stephens's crew has come out to the set a couple of times, even. That could explain why he looks a little familiar to me." Her gaze fixated in the distance. "Did he say why he was here? He's not looking for me, is he? How would he know I'm here? He couldn't know I was here."

Nate shook his head. "I didn't get the impression he was looking for you, just that he'd stumbled upon you. I'm not sure, though. You feel pretty confident that he's not your stalker?"

Kylie's pensive expression returned. "He lives in New York and produces a daily cooking show. I'd have a hard time believing it could be him." She tucked a hair behind her ear. "Should I go say something?"

"That depends. Do you want your show to go national?"

"I think so. I don't know."

"If you go talk to him, he's going to want to know why you're waitressing at a restaurant here in York-town. What would you tell him?"

She shook her head as if cold water had just been thrown at her. "Of course. You're right. I'll just get the soup ready and let you serve them. There are more important things right now than my show. First, I've got to put a nightmare to rest behind bars."

Nate could see she was frazzled and tried to offer a reassuring smile. "Okay, two bowls of crab soup."

"Got it." She grabbed two bowls and ladled the creamy soup into their depths. She placed them on a tray and handed them to Nate.

Nate tried to keep a cool head as he stepped back into the dining area. He couldn't let down his guard yet. It seemed too big a coincidence that the Cuisine TV producer just happened to show up at his restaurant while Kylie was here. He'd be cautious.

"Here we go. Two bowls of my dad's famous crab soup and some freshly baked bread." Nate set the food on the table. He brought the tray to his side and looked at the men. "Can I get you anything else?"

"This smells delicious. I think we'll be fine," Arnold answered.

Nate paused before walking away. "If you don't

mind me asking, what brings you to Yorktown? To The Revolutionary Grill for that matter?"

"I'm always scouting out new restaurants for different shows at the network. This week, I'm hitting the Historic Triangle, as I believe you locals call it. Yorktown, Jamestown and Williamsburg."

"I'm honored you chose to come here."

"Your place caught my eye right away. It's got a great location with the river out front, and I like the theming." He held up a spoonful of soup. "Now I'm ready to try your food."

Nate nodded toward him. "I'll let you do that. I'll be back in a few minutes to see if you need anything else."

Nate walked away, feeling in his gut that this guy knew more than he'd let on.

10

Kylie couldn't get the man's face out of her mind as she finished the rest of her lunch. Nate, who would normally have disappeared into his office, since the dining room was so slow, instead cleaned the already clean kitchen. Kylie knew he purposely stayed close.

From where Kylie sat, she could hear the two men outside chatting, though she couldn't make out their words. If Larry found out that she'd run into Arnold and didn't make an effort to be noticed, he would be angry. Oh, well. She'd learned long ago not to let Larry get to her. He was just doing his job as producer. Meanwhile, she had to look out for herself.

She took another bite of her chef salad and chewed slowly.

Arnold Stephens's face flashed in her mind. The fact that the man had shown up here was just a coincidence. It had to be. But was the world really this small? And did coincidences like this really happen?

"Excuse me," a deep voice said from the distance.

Kylie's head snapped up and she saw Arnold peering in from the doorway. She wiped her mouth and stood quickly, her chair tumbling behind her with the action. In a flash, Nate was by her side.

"Can I help you?" Nate said.

"This soup is fabulous."

Nate slapped his dish towel over his shoulder and stepped closer. "Thanks. I appreciate that."

Arnold's gaze went back to Kylie. He slowly nodded to her and then smiled. "You are Kylie Summers. I've watched videos of your show for the past several weeks. I remember your face. And I know you're on vacation this week because I called your producer last Friday."

Kylie had only a minute to decide on her reaction. Own up to his declaration or deny it. Tell the truth or lie. She'd never believed that lying was the best option—an option at all, for that matter. But would the truth put her in danger? Nate looked over at her, clearly showing that he'd left the ball in her court.

She drew in a deep breath. "I am Kylie, Mr. Stephens. I'm simply trying not to draw any attention to myself while I'm here in Yorktown."

"I see. That's admirable, I suppose. But I have a proposition for you."

Kylie braced herself, placing her hands palm down on the table. "A proposition?"

"I love the look and location of this restaurant. I love the crab soup. And I love *Kylie's Kitchen.* What do you say we do a pilot episode of your show, right here at The Revolutionary Grill? I can't think of a more winning combination. We're looking to film right away."

Kylie opened her mouth to speak, but nothing came out. A national debut? Giving the restaurant a chance at a free advertisement to a huge audience?

"You want to give me a chance? Go national?"

Mr. Stephens smiled, his teeth practically sparkling. "I believe in fate, and I think fate is why I ended up here today. Yes, we are interested in taking your show national."

"That sounds great."

Nate stepped forward. "Kylie . . . I don't know if that's a good idea right now."

What was he talking about? Of course this was a good idea. For both her and Nate's restaurant. "It sounds like a good idea to me."

He leaned close, so close that she could feel his breath on her cheek. "Remember why you're here."

Reality settled in. Of course she couldn't film now. Not until everything with the stalker was resolved. She couldn't assume that the sting would go as planned and that she would be back home by next week at this time.

"Think about it." Arnold handed her a business card. "I'll be in town until the end of the week. I really think this could be a win-win situation for all of us."

He offered a clipped nod, one that spoke confidence and determination. Then he dropped some money at the register and left.

Kylie turned to Nate after the door clicked shut.

"I think I was blinded by ambition there for a moment."

"It would have been a great opportunity. If it's meant to be, Mr. Stephens will come around again— at a better time."

Kylie nodded. Nate was right. She had to wait on the right timing. Her first priority was to catch her stalker. But if this was the right decision, why did her heart feel so heavy?

The bell chimed above the door, signaling the arrival of another patron. Kylie sucked in a deep breath. "I'll go seat them."

Nate got back to his apartment exhausted yet revitalized. He and Kylie had made a decent team and they'd somehow survived the frantic day. It was both a blessing and a curse that business had been slow. They probably wouldn't have been able to handle many more customers, though it would have been nice for the restaurant's bottom line.

Out of curiosity, he plopped down at his computer desk and typed "Kylie's Kitchen" into his search engine. Pages of results came up. He clicked on the official site for the show.

A moment later, Kylie's glowing face filled the screen. He examined her photo. Her pert nose, big eyes, tiny chin. Her long, dark hair flowing halfway down her back. Her smooth skin and easy smile. No doubt she was easy on the eyes. That didn't always translate into being a good TV personality, however.

He clicked on a link to one of her show's episodes.

A cheery song introduced the show before the camera zoomed in on a bright, clean kitchen, equipped with all the modern necessities and perfect lighting. Kylie stood behind an enlarged kitchen island with a variety of fruits and vegetables in front of her, along with a chopping board and butcher knife. Her warm smile greeted viewers and invited them into her haven.

Nate leaned back in his chair as she began sharing a simple recipe for chicken cordon bleu with garlic mashed potatoes. She had a way of engaging her audience by sharing stories about growing up and restaurants she'd visited that inspired her and local markets where she'd found a treasure of fresh foods. By the end of the show, she nearly had Nate convinced.

If only Nate shared her passion for food.

He glanced at the wall where he'd hung up a picture of himself shaking hands with the President of the United States when he'd been awarded a Medal of Honor. He'd saved somewhere around a dozen passengers on a tour boat that almost sank off the coast of North Carolina and he'd nearly lost his own life in the process.

The boat should have never been out with the storm approaching. But his job hadn't been to judge, just to help. At thirty-eight-years old, as a decorated master chief petty officer, he'd been given the choice to advance or to retire. Against his better judgment, he'd chosen early retirement so he could honor his father's dying wish to keep the restaurant going. If it wasn't for the pension he received each month, he would have had to close down months ago.

A quiet knock sounded at his door. Since the outside doors were locked, the only person it could be at this hour was Kylie, and Nate had assumed she would have fallen right to sleep after working so hard today. He yanked the door open, concerned that something might be wrong.

Kylie stood on the other side, her eyes red-rimmed as if she'd been crying. Her shoulders appeared hunched, her breaths labored.

"Kylie," he mumbled. "Come in. Please."

As she shuffled inside, Nate's gut lurched. He took her arm and led her across the room to the couch. "Do you want something to drink? Coffee?"

She sank into the couch and brought her hands up under her chin. "No, thanks. I'm sorry to bother you."

He lowered himself into a chair across from her. "You're not bothering me."

She wiped her eyes with a tissue that had been balled in her hand. "My brother just called. They've canceled the sting. They don't know when they'll be able to do it now. The cop who was supposed to double for me took a spill while chasing a suspect during a robbery. She fractured her wrists, which will make it hard for her to chop up food."

"When do they think this cop will be able to do the demonstration still, if they're even able to reschedule it?"

Kylie shrugged. "It depends on how long it takes her to recover. The longer we wait, the more likely my stalker will figure out the person at the demonstration isn't me. Time isn't on our side in this case."

"I'm sorry, Kylie." He looked at her sitting alone on the couch. What would it be like to sit beside her and pull her into his arms, to comfort her? No, soon she'd be leaving. Besides, she despised Nate's efforts to protect her. No doubt she'd feel the same if he tried to comfort her.

"Me, too." She looked in the distance, tension still present around her eyes and mouth. "I'm going to have to call my producer and let him know I'm extending my 'vacation' for a bit longer. He won't be happy, especially not now that Arnold Stephens has called again."

"He'll get over it."

Kylie remained silent, pensive.

"Do you want a national cooking show, Kylie?"

Kylie's lips pulled into a tight line before she finally spoke. "I do. I mean, there are some things I'm still unsure about." She paused and shook her head. "I know I sound crazy, but I'll probably have to move to New York, and I've never been a big city type of girl. Those types of things cause some uncertainty. But do you know how many people dream about having a nationally syndicated show? I'd be crazy to pass the opportunity up."

And maybe it would finally show her family that she was truly a "grown-up" and that they didn't need to treat her like a child anymore. Of course, the measures of success she'd already achieved hadn't done the trick.

"It does sound like a great opportunity."

"When I was diagnosed with cancer, I realized how short life was. I want to take advantage of each opportunity and live life to the fullest. But it's like I've told you, I haven't taken a vacation in years, so I haven't mastered the whole 'living life to the fullest' yet either."

"Life is a journey. We learn as we go."

She stood and sighed, almost as if she didn't want to leave. "I know you're probably anxious for me to go so you can resume your life."

Nate stood and reached for her arm. "Kylie, I don't know what I would have done today without you. You can stay here for as long as you need to stay. Understand?"

Her cheeks flushed before she looked away. "Thanks, Nate. I appreciate all you've done."

He squeezed her arm, realizing he didn't want to let go—right now or ever.

Back in her apartment, Kylie sank into the couch, replaying her conversation with Nate. He was a surprisingly good listener. His encouragement to follow her own heart had warmed her in surprising ways.

She'd expected Nate to react more like Colin would have, telling her what she *should* be feeling and how she *should* be handling the situation. Strangely, she hadn't even realized how controlling he'd been until many months into their relationship. How could she have been so blind? Why would she ever even try to be someone she wasn't just to please a boyfriend?

The thought shamed her.

Colin had wanted someone who'd do whatever he said, who would be a quiet, compliant wife who always stood by his side and never talked back. Kylie wasn't that person. She dreamed of a balanced marriage that was built on mutual respect, where listening to each other's opinions was a priority. She'd hold out until she found that.

In the meantime, she'd vowed to never let a man control her again. Yet that was exactly what the Man in Black was doing. His very presence sent her into a nervous scurry, even being this far away

He couldn't find her here.

But could he?

Crazier things had happened in life. For instance, Arnold Stephens, of all people, coming into the Grill today. She'd known the world was small, but was it really this small?

Mr. Stephens couldn't be her stalker . . . could he?

She shook her head. No, that idea was crazy. He was a successful producer living in New York City. No way he could be behind the threats on her life.

Finally, her muscles began relaxing from the

busy day. With a sigh, she rose and decided it was time for bed. After checking the closet and under the bed, plus going back to double-check the locks on her door again, she finally crawled under the covers. She wished for a good night's rest, but a good night's rest was something she hadn't experienced in months.

11

Carrie was out again on Thursday because of the flu. It looked like she'd be out for several days, for that matter.

Suzy did come in on Thursday, which was a help, but they were still at least one person short. Kylie only hoped that Nate had a plan for the weekend, which was always busier. Being short-staffed on Friday night would be a nightmare.

Thursday, so far, had passed by fairly quickly. Kylie needed to keep her mind occupied, and being in the kitchen did just that. She tried to keep it to where she was cooking and Nate worked on the management side.

She couldn't resist throwing in a few personal touches to the food while Nate was in the office. Just a little parsley here and lemon juice or zest there. The additions helped to brighten up the flavors.

She had some ideas for new menu items she thought Nate should try—and other ideas for menu items that he should do away with. At the right time, maybe she would suggest them.

"What did you do to this soup?" Suzy walked into the kitchen and held up an empty bowl.

Kylie drew in a quick breath, hoping she didn't do something wrong. "I just added a couple of extra ingredients."

"It's fabulous."

Kylie smiled. "Thanks. It just needed a little extra something to take it to the next level."

"The customers have been raving about it all afternoon."

"Glad to hear that."

Suzy leaned against the sink, adjusting the purple bandanna with little skull imprints that she wore around her head like a pirate—not in trying to keep with any theme, just because she seemed to like standing out in the crowd. "You're not new at this, are you?"

Kylie tensed. "What do you mean?"

"Nate said you came here to get experience, but you seem pretty experienced to me."

Kylie shrugged, trying to look casual. "I'm trying to get restaurant experience. I've had some training as a chef."

"Why'd you pick this restaurant of all places to get experience?"

She lowered her voice as her eyes darted from side to side. "There are some fabulous places up in Williamsburg. I'd hardly call this place inspirational."

Kylie swallowed, her throat dry. A customer right now would be nice, before Suzy had a chance to ask too many questions. Kylie shoved a lock of hair behind her ear and put on her best game face. "You sound like you know quite a bit about the restaurant industry yourself."

Suzy shrugged, seeming more than eager to switch the subject to herself. "I don't know. I've been waitressing for six years now, ever since I was seventeen. I'm taking some college classes in between, you know. I've worked nearly every place from here to Jamestown."

"How'd you end up here, then?"

"My dad goes to church with Nate and knew he needed some help." She shrugged again and pursed her lips in nonchalance. "This place is closer to home anyway, so it saves me some gas money. The tips aren't nearly as good, though."

"It's nice of you to help Nate out. You don't go to church with your dad?"

"I gave up on church a long time ago." She waved her hand in the air as if to show the question was invalid. "I believe in God and everything. But I don't need church to show it."

Kylie nodded, guilt pooling in her gut. Hearing Suzy say the words out loud made her realize how feeble her own arguments against going to church sounded. She needed to get back in the habit. Yet, at the same time, she didn't want to go to church simply out of habit.

Instead of talking about it further, Kylie changed the subject. "So, what are you studying and taking classes for?"

Suzy shrugged again. "I can't decide, so I'm trying a little bit of everything. I just want something that will take me away from this place. I've been praying a rich man would come along and sweep me off my feet, take me off to a better life. Hasn't happened yet." She frowned dramatically.

"You don't like Yorktown?"

"I've lived here since I was born, and there's nothing left for me here except my family, I guess. All this historical stuff is spooky to me anyway. It seems like every place around here is supposedly haunted, my house included. In fact, they even talk about it on the ghost tour. I'm so proud."

Kylie smiled. "What about this place? Does it have a story, too?"

Suzy leaned toward her. "The only thing haunting this place is Nate. You'd think his father was still here. He needs to just sell the place. He's miserable. I hate to see him like that. He used to actually have some life in him."

"Doing something you don't love can do that to you, I suppose."

The bell jangled on the front door and Suzy straightened. "I gotta go. Good talking to you. You're good for this place, Kylie. I don't know why you chose to come here, but I'm glad you did."

Kylie watched her walk away before turning back to her work area and preparing for her next order. But her mind was on Nate. If there was one thing she'd learned from having lymphoma, it was that life was too short to do something you didn't love doing. What would it take for Nate to realize that?

The day had gone fairly smoothly, all things considered. But the weekend was nearly upon them and business always picked up on the weekends. Nate wasn't sure what he'd do without Carrie here to help out.

He sighed and leaned back in his desk chair in his cramped little office. His ex-girlfriend Deanna used to help him in the restaurant, but she'd been unreliable. She always had some kind of emergency come up where she'd need his help right then. And of course he'd always dropped everything to help her. He hadn't minded helping; in fact, he'd wanted to help.

But he'd realized that she'd been using him. Their relationship had been one-sided, with her doing all the taking and Nate doing all the giving.

She'd needed rescuing, and Nate had been more than happy to do the job. What he hadn't realized at the time was that she was one of those people who clung to their rescuer and nearly pulled them underwater also.

The two had met when Nate accidentally clipped her car while parking. The scrape was minor, but she'd been in tears. Nate had offered to fix her car, since she didn't have insurance and Nate didn't want to get his insurance company involved.

A week later, when her car had broken down on

the side of the road, she'd called Nate for help. That evening, they had coffee and she explained that she was new in town and looking for a job. Said she'd been running from a hopeless situation back home and needed a new start. Nate had fallen for it all. He'd even stuck with her when he discovered that the hopeless situation was that her boss had fired her from the department store for embezzling money. The money she'd needed for a dying grandma back home had simply been pocketed. Her grandmother had passed away years ago.

He hadn't found any of this out until Deanna had disappeared one day and he went looking for her, worried that something was wrong. That's when all the ugly truths had been discovered. He hadn't actually found Deanna, but he'd found people from her past who'd filled him in.

He'd eventually heard through the grapevine that she'd taken up with a wealthy businessman she'd met at The Revolutionary Grill. She'd moved up to Richmond with him and was now enjoying the indulgent lifestyle she'd always desired.

Never again would he be taken for a fool. He didn't mind helping out the occasional damsel in distress, but never again would he date one. Never again would he trust one, for that matter.

Kylie stuck her head in the door. "Have you given any thought to what you'll do tomorrow? Carrie probably won't be up for coming in."

"Yeah, I've thought about that. Haven't come up with any great ideas, though."

"There's always Harvey . . ."

"Harvey knows nothing about working in a restaurant."

"But he's great with people. That's all you need for someone who's greeting patrons, seating them and bringing them water. I think he'd be a great choice."

Nate scowled. "He's too old to be on his feet all day."

"He'd disagree. He has more energy than any twenty-year-old I know." She stepped back. "Think about it."

She started to walk away when Nate called to her. She turned in his direction.

Nate had to ask a question that had been on his mind. He leaned back in his chair, trying to appear casual. "Kylie, have you been changing my recipes?"

The guilt he saw in her frown gave him his answer.

His chin jutted out. "I appreciate your eagerness

to help, but our customers like our dishes the way they are."

Kylie's frown disappeared and fire ignited in her eyes. "Your customers are mostly tourists who come here once on vacation and never come back."

Tension pinched his back. "That's not true. I have regulars. And they've noticed some changes lately. I appreciate your enthusiasm and your help, but I didn't bring you here to improve my menu or give me advice. I brought you here to . . . to keep you safe."

Kylie scowled. "I was just trying to help. You know, if you just made a few simple changes, it could make a big difference."

He held up a hand. "Save it, Kylie. I've got enough on my plate now as it is. The last thing I need is to mix up things here."

She held up her hands in what appeared to be surrender. "I think you're making a mistake, but fine. This isn't my restaurant, so I shouldn't care one way or another. Besides, with any luck, I'll be leaving soon."

Why did her last statement feel like a slap in the face? Nate didn't have time to figure it out now.

"I'd like to take my dinner break now. Is it okay if I use your computer?"

He reached into his pocket. "You can use the one in my apartment."

Kylie didn't smile when she took his keys. "Thanks."

When she was out of sight, Nate let his head drop back onto the chair. Women. Why did they have to be so complicated?

Kylie stomped upstairs. Why couldn't Nate simply appreciate her opinions? Listen to her suggestions? Taste the improvements she'd made to his soups and salads? Why did he have to be so hardheaded?

She jammed the key into the lock and opened the door to Nate's apartment. Standing in the doorway, Kylie's gaze wandered the place freely. Typical bachelor pad, she decided. Coast Guard memorabilia hanging on the wall by the computer caught her eye.

Crossing the room, Kylie examined it. The light in Nate's eyes was different in these pictures. He should still be in the Coast Guard instead of making himself miserable trying to run a restaurant that he despised.

She shook her head and plopped down in a

rickety computer chair. It wasn't like Nate would ever listen to her opinion anyway. She turned the computer on, and a moment later it had booted up. The Web page for *Kylie's Kitchen* appeared on the screen. Kylie raised her eyebrows.

So, Nate had been checking out her show? She shouldn't care and scolded herself for the joy she'd quickly felt.

Shaking her head, she navigated to the show's message board. A string of messages from FAN756 popped up. Kylie sucked in a breath as her gaze scanned them.

"We need some new episodes of *Kylie's Kitchen.* I heard she's not taping right now and wonder why. Anyone know?" Someone replied that Kylie was on vacation.

FAN756 replied, "I wonder where she went. The Caribbean? The mountains? New York City?"

Others speculated various other places, based on restaurants and travels she'd mentioned on air. Thankfully, they were all wrong.

The next thread was about the cooking demonstration scheduled for today.

Someone wrote, "Kylie's cooking demonstration canceled for today. Too bad. I miss seeing her beautiful face. Anyone know if she's appearing anywhere else instead?"

Kylie mouth dropped open when her home address flashed across the screen. "You can find her here, although she might not appreciate you dropping by unexpectedly. LOL."

How had they found her home address? And why in the world would someone post it online? Were they insane?

Her brother knew about FAN756. Whoever this person was, he remained at the top of the police's suspect list. If only they could trace this person's identity. The person posted from different locations and never from a computer that required logging in.

Kylie shuddered. She'd tell her brother about the messages and have him call Larry to remove her home address from the site. What else could she do at this point?

She glanced at her watch. She had to get back down to the restaurant in a few minutes. Quickly, she logged on to her email account and braced herself for whatever she might find.

Most of the messages were from FAN756 and stated the same things as had been written in the forum. She forwarded them all to her brother.

Kylie focused on the rest of her emails. Larry, her

producer, had sent her several emails claiming they needed to talk. Nothing but his normal "Larry" diatribe. Where was she? He needed her back. New opportunities had popped up. Blah, blah, blah. She shot him an email back reminding him that she was on a well-deserved vacation and everything could wait until she returned.

There was one final email from an unknown sender. She hesitated before clicking on it. A video popped onto the screen of Kylie cooking on her set. She recognized it as an old episode of *Kylie's Kitchen.* Except this time, the oven exploded and Kylie's face melted like wax down the screen as flames ate away at her.

Kylie gasped. At the end of the video, the words "Come out, come out, wherever you are" scrolled across the screen.

Fear clenched her spine. She squeezed her eyes shut as the taunt replayed in her mind. Would this nightmare ever end?

ylie hurried to her apartment and called her brother, telling him to watch for the emails she'd forwarded. Maybe the police back home could figure out who they'd come from. It was doubtful. They hadn't figured out any of the emails sent to her before.

Why had she clicked on that unknown email? Sending threatening notes was one thing, but creating a video that showed her dying was another. An ice-cold shiver ran down her spine as she mentally replayed the oven exploding.

A picture formed in her mind of the person behind these threats. Based on his grammar, his computer skills, his video skills and his knack for never leaving any clues, she pictured him to be well educated, professional, maybe even successful.

Colin? She shook her head, praying he wasn't behind this. He'd been a control freak, but he wouldn't stoop this low. Would he?

Or what about Arnold Stephens? He certainly had the know-how and even the money to do whatever he wanted. And he'd shown up here in Yorktown. Was that really a coincidence?

Could either Colin or Arnold secretly be FAN756?

The possibilities only gave Kylie a headache.

She decided to go downstairs.

"You done with your break?" Suzy asked.

"Yeah, why don't you go ahead and take yours?"

"You'll get no arguments from me."

As she walked back into the kitchen, the bell over the door jangled. She grabbed a menu and went into the dining room to play hostess.

An attractive, dark-haired man walked toward the kitchen. She tensed as he approached.

"Hey, is Nate in?" He tapped his knuckles against the counter, seeming to sense her apprehension. "Sorry, I didn't see you there. Didn't mean to scare you."

"He's in his office. Can I help you?"

"I'm a friend. John. I just wanted to stop by and tell him hello."

Kylie nodded, still not at ease. "I'll go tell him." Just as she reached his office, Nate pulled the door open and stepped out.

"John! Glad you could come by. Sit down and we'll get you something to eat."

Kylie watched the exchange, surprised by Nate's sudden warmth. Nate flipped his hand toward her. "Kylie, this is one of my old Coast Guard buddies, John. John, this is Kylie. She's helping me out here at the restaurant for a few days."

John smiled again and squeezed Nate's shoulder in some type of male camaraderie. "Nice to meet you, Kylie. Old Nate here can use all the help he can get."

The two men laughed before sitting down at a table by the window. Kylie drew in a deep breath and decided to put the email behind her for now. After she excused herself, she heard John say something about the Coast Guard Training Center. No wonder Nate had perked up when he saw the man. John was apparently Nate's link to doing what he was passionate about.

Kylie passed the window in front of the restaurant and paused. There, across the street, standing on the beach. She squinted. Was that Arnold Stephens? What was he doing back in Yorktown? And why was he standing outside The Revolutionary Grill?

Just at that moment, he turned, looked at her and smiled. Fear sizzled up her spine. Beside her, she was vaguely aware of someone saying her name. A strong hand clamped around her arm and nudged her. Her eyes remained fixated on the man smiling at her from the beach.

Nate's voice rang out again. "Kylie?"

With a trembling hand, she pointed outside. "It's Arnold Stephens. On the beach. Watching the restaurant."

Nate's lips pulled into a thin line. "John, stay with Kylie." Before his friend could respond, Nate charged out the door and toward Arnold. John took quick strides to join her. "What's going on?" he asked.

"It's just that man outside . . ."

"Is he giving you trouble?"

Kylie shrugged. "Maybe."

Kylie watched from the window as Nate confronted Arnold. The producer threw his arms up in the air and Kylie imagined that he proclaimed his innocence.

The next thing Kylie knew, Nate was dragging him by the collar back toward the restaurant. Kylie squeezed her eyes closed, pinching the bridge of her nose. She was strong enough to face her stalker. She could do this.

The bell jangled and Nate pushed Arnold inside. John stood guard on the other side of the producer.

"He said he was about to come back in here and ask if you'd considered his request to film here." Nate still grasped Arnold by the collar of his expensive shirt.

"I had no ill intentions." Arnold held up his hands. "I decided to enjoy the view for a moment before coming inside."

"Why have you been following Kylie?" Nate demanded.

"Following Kylie? I've been following her show for months, if that's what you mean. I've simply been trying to figure out if we want to take her on as a new show on Cuisine TV. Nothing evil about that."

"How'd you know she was in Yorktown?"

"I didn't. Not until I wandered into this fine establishment." He straightened, trying to shrug away from Nate. "What's going on here? Most chefs who want to make it big would love to have my attention."

Kylie tried to take control of the situation, but her trembling voice belied her act. "Can you verify where you've been over the past two weeks, Mr. Stephens?"

"Certainly. I'll get my assistant to bring you my calendar."

"Have you been in Kentucky at all?"

"Kentucky?" His eyebrows shot up as if the idea were absurd. "Of course not. Why would I go back to Kentucky?"

If he hadn't been in Kentucky, then he couldn't have ransacked her place.

Kylie licked her lips, trying to remain calm. "I'd like to see that calendar."

"I can even do better. I can provide you with the names and numbers of people I've been in contact with over the past fourteen days." His gaze flickered from Nate, to Kylie, to John. "Now, can someone tell me what's going on?"

Nate's gaze rested on Kylie, leaving the decision to her. "Someone's been stalking me for the past several months, Mr. Stephens. I'm here in Yorktown to lie low for a while until they catch the man who's been terrorizing me."

His bottom lip dropped down. "Why, that's awful. No wondered you reacted the way you did. But I assure you, I am not that man. I am a fan of yours, but I'd never want to scare someone I'm trying to recruit. That would be ludicrous."

Nate put a hand on his hip, not lowering his guard even a touch. "So, you're telling me you had no idea Kylie was here when you wandered in last week?"

Arnold shrugged rather sheepishly. "Well, I did have a small clue. Someone from Kentucky who watches you there called me and said they'd spotted you here in Yorktown. I was curious as to what you were up to. I just had to come and see for myself. But, you see, I'd been wanting a tour of this area for quite some time. If I'd known about the circumstances around you coming here, I would have never done so."

"Someone from Kentucky recognized me here?" A tremble coursed through Kylie. "They didn't say anything to me. Why would they call you?"

"They said one of my shows was on while they were dining." He nodded toward a TV in the corner. "I posted something at the end of the show about looking for new talent. Something just clicked in this woman's head, I suppose. I didn't think anything of it."

Kylie shook her head, feeling overwhelmed

again. "Mr. Stephens, please call your assistant and ask him to come. I'd like to speak with him alone, please."

Mr. Stephens's story checked out, and he left with the promise that Kylie could still be in touch once her stalker was behind bars.

Yeah, right. She had about as much of a chance to get on Cuisine TV as a high schooler working in a fast-food joint. Her dreams crashed around her, leaving her heart heavy.

Nate plopped down in a chair beside her in the dining area. Mr. Stephens had left and Suzy clocked out for the night.

"Are you okay?" The steadiness of Nate's gaze showed Kylie that she had all of his focus and concern.

She had to tell him about the email she'd received earlier. "Someone sent me a video they'd made of me . . . well, of me basically melting . . . when an oven explodes. It's put me on edge. I guess I'm suspicious of everyone now. Even your friend John, when he first walked in."

She wished she had a friend to hug her, to tell her that everything was okay. At the moment, she could relate to a buoy floating alone in the middle of the sea.

As if Nate could read her mind, he scooted his chair closer and pulled her toward his chest. His arms felt strong and stable around her. Though her body relaxed, her heart sped.

"It's going to be okay, Kylie. This will all be over soon," he murmured.

"I hate feeling like this, Nate."

"Anybody in your situation would feel like you do. I'm sorry you're going through this, and I wish I could lift more of your burden."

She raised her head and saw his intense gaze. "You mean that, don't you?"

"Of course I do."

She put her head back against his chest. For a moment— just a moment—she wanted to relish feeling safe.

And even though Nate was just being kind, she willed her heart to stop pounding uncontrollably at his closeness.

The next morning, Nate looked at his watch for the fifteenth time in that many minutes. Today would be busy, and he'd been counting on Suzy coming in early to help with some prep. She'd volunteered for the task last night, probably to make up for not answering her phone the day when they'd been short-staffed.

As soon as Kylie stepped into the kitchen, still blinking back signs of sleepiness, Nate stopped rolling silverware into napkins and turned toward her. He'd heard the two ladies chatting in the kitchen yesterday, though he couldn't make out what it was about. Maybe Suzy had decided to communicate with Kylie instead of calling Nate. Stranger things had happened.

But as soon as he saw Kylie, he remembered the trauma she'd felt last night and tried to soften his voice. "How are you doing today?"

She nodded. "Better. Thanks."

Nate wasn't so sure, but he'd have to take her word for now. "Have you, by chance, heard from Suzy?"

Kylie stared at him uncertainly for a moment, still blinking like she needed more coffee before processing his question. "Suzy? Have I heard from her? No. Why?"

Nate shook his head, frustration mounting at his temples. "She's not here, which is unusual. Getting her to come in on her day off is next to impossible, but for her not to show up on a day she's scheduled to work is not like her."

Kylie seemed to relax a bit. "Have you called her?"

"She's not answering her cell phone," Nate mumbled. He glanced around the kitchen, trying to decide on his next course of action. He needed Suzy to be here today, and if she was still sleeping, he'd have to wake her up, even if it meant calling her parents. "I'll try her dad. Maybe he knows where she is. There's just absolutely no way to handle tonight's crowd without her here."

He walked into the office and flipped through his rolodex until he found Suzy's father's phone number at work. A minute later, Simon, her father, answered the phone. Nate explained that he was looking for Suzy.

Simon sighed, the noise mounding like it was born out of weariness more than anger. "No, Suzy didn't come home last night, Nate. I have no idea where she is. I wish I did, so I could remind her about the rules of still living at home at her age. She may be old enough to be an adult, but if she's living in our house, she has to abide by our rules."

Nate put a hand to his hip while gripping the

phone with his other hand. "She didn't come home last night? At all?"

"No, but she does that every once in a while. I wish she wouldn't, but you know how these young people can be. Her mother and I have told her that if she continues, she's going to have to find a place of her own. I'd hate to actually do it, but that's what it's looking like."

"She's not at work yet. It's very unlike her."

Simon paused. "If she's not there by ten, let me know. I'll see what I can do. My guess is that she had a little too much fun partying last night, went to a friend's house and overslept." The catch of concern in his voice belied his simple explanation.

"Got it, Simon. I'll be in touch." Nate hung up and ran a hand through his hair as he glanced over his office, feeling a bit overwhelmed at the prospect of opening today with just Kylie and himself staffing the restaurant. He had to hire some more workers. But could his budget handle it? He supposed it would have to. Being half-staffed was no way to attract customers. It was no way to even stay open, for that matter.

"What's wrong?" Kylie leaned in the doorway with her arms crossed over her chest. From her stance, Nate would guess that she'd been there the whole time and had heard half of the conversation.

Nate let out a brief sigh. "Suzy didn't go home last night, but apparently that's not unusual. Her dad thinks she'll get here eventually. He said she's been hanging out with some partying types lately and they've got her acting a little irresponsible."

Kylie rubbed her arms with her hands as if she was cold. "She's never done anything like this before?"

Nate shook his head. "Never."

"Maybe she'll show up soon."

"Yeah, well, in the meantime, it looks like I'm going to have to take your suggestion and call Harvey. I'm running out of options."

She cleared her throat. "I have another option, if you're open to it."

"I'm open to anything right now."

"How about doing a buffet? I'm a caterer. I know how to put together big meals for big crowds. We can take some of the staples from here in the restaurant and make them in big batches. That way we need less manpower up front."

"I like that idea, Kylie. I really like that idea. Make whatever you want. The Revolutionary Grill is going to do something new today."

Kylie nodded, looking a little too pleased that he'd taken her suggestion. He ignored her small smile and picked up the phone again.

Harvey agreed—seemed thrilled, even—to help out at the restaurant, and Darlene seemed equally thrilled to have him out of the house.

He arrived at the restaurant less than ten minutes after Nate called him. Kylie showed him the ropes while Nate continued to prep the kitchen area. The sound of Harvey's cheery voice in the dining area made Nate think that Kylie had been right.

Harvey might make a great fill-in today. He sure hoped so. The restaurant wouldn't survive much longer under these conditions.

At eleven o'clock, when the doors opened and Suzy was still nowhere to be found, Nate called Simon again. This time, his friend's concern was more obvious. His voice sounded strained.

"You're right, that's not like her to not be there yet, Nate." Simon sighed, weariness evident in his voice. "I was really hoping she'd show up. Let me make some calls and I'll be back in touch."

Nate's gut twisted and he wanted to somehow fix the situation but knew he couldn't. At this point, there was very little he could do to help, even. "Can I do anything, Simon?"

"Just let me know if you hear from her. Most likely, she's just being irresponsible. But let me check with her friends, just to be on the safe side." He paused again. "I hope she's just being irresponsible."

He tried to put Suzy's disappearance out of his mind as customers began coming in. As they worked, Nate noted that Kylie seemed quieter than normal. Nate had to wonder if Suzy was on her mind. With everything else that had been going on in Kylie's life, something like this could likely freak her out, make her mind go places it shouldn't.

Nate would keep an eye on her today especially. Her emotional state still seemed fragile, and the last thing Nate wanted was for Kylie to reach her breaking point.

After the lunch crowd passed, Kylie paused to catch a breath. Suzy had been on her mind all morning. Certainly, the girl was simply being irresponsible. Just yesterday she'd told Kylie that she was praying for some rich gentleman to sweep her off her feet and get her out of this town. Maybe that had happened? She rubbed her temples to ease the pounding there.

Kylie didn't know the girl that well, but somehow, she doubted that was the case. She continued to make a Cornwallis Corned Beef, complete with rustic bread, freshly sliced meat and gooey melted cheese.

Nate worked the station behind her, saying very little. Maybe that was good. She didn't have much to say, and the thoughts that did sweep through her mind would only make her sound paranoid. Instead, Kylie chose to work silently, only asking questions about orders or yelling when a meal was up.

From the door to the kitchen, a deep, masculine voice called Nate's name. Kylie turned to see who'd arrived and spotted a man with smooth skin but a shock of white hair that made him appear possibly older. The serious look in the man's eyes instantly concerned Kylie.

"Simon." Nate walked briskly toward the man, his shoulders looking rigid as he approached. "Any word from Suzy?"

The man shook his head, worry showing in the dullness of the man's eyes. "No, none of her friends have heard from her. The best I can tell, you both were the last ones to speak with her. Did she mention going anywhere after work last night?"

"Not to me." Nate turned to Kylie. "Did Suzy say anything to you about doing anything last night?"

Kylie shook her head, wishing she could offer something. "No, my impression was that she was going home. She said she was tired and that her feet hurt from working the long shift."

The man's chin dropped down toward his chest. "I just thought I'd check here first to make sure she didn't show up. I'm going to go tell the sheriff, report her as a missing person. They probably won't be able to do anything yet, but my gut tells me that something's wrong."

"Simon, is there anything I can do?" Nate stepped forward. "Anything at all?"

"Just pray."

After he left, Nate and Kylie stood in silence. Finally, Kylie cleared her throat. "I hope she's okay."

"Yorktown isn't known for its crime, unless you count the occasional vandalism. The chances of something happening to her here are highly unlikely."

Kylie couldn't decide if he'd directed that statement toward the situation with Suzy or if he was speaking about Kylie's stalker. Either way, Kylie hoped his words were true. She hoped Suzy was okay.

Shortly after seven, an older man with a slow gait and perceptive eyes walked into the restaurant. Nate introduced him to Kylie as Detective Blackston.

"I know Simon already talked to you, but I just wanted to ask a few questions also about Suzy," Detective Blackston said. "It's too early to consider her a missing person, but we want to go ahead and get some preliminary information."

"We'll be happy to help in any way possible," Nate said.

"I also wanted to let you know that Suzy's car is still in the parking lot out back. After she left here, she must have gotten a ride with someone else to wherever she is now, or walked. I have investigators out there now, looking for any clues as to where she might be."

Kylie sucked in a breath. Things were looking more and more suspicious. She prayed Suzy was okay.

"Did Suzy mention anything at all yesterday that might have given you the impression she wasn't going home?" The detective waited with pad poised in hand.

Should Kylie mention the tidbit Suzy had told her about wanting to get out of this town? Kylie decided that every detail could be important.

"The only thing she mentioned yesterday to me was that she'd like to be swept away one day by a rich man who'd take her away from this place," said Kylie. "But she probably said that at three o'clock, so it doesn't seem likely it happened between then and the time she left."

"Were there any customers here who were acting strangely?" Blackston asked.

Arnold Stephens's face flashed in her mind. Kylie couldn't imagine the producer harming Suzy, but had he swept her away? He was handsome and had money. He wasn't from around here, from New York City, as a matter of fact. Kylie shook the thought away. No, it didn't seem likely that she'd somehow met up with him and they'd run off together. But again, any detail could be important. She should let the sheriff decide what was of relevance to her disappearance and what was not.

"Ms. Summers?"

Kylie blinked out of her thoughts and saw the detective staring at her. She glanced at Nate, searching his face for a sign of what she should say. He nodded, as if reading her thoughts.

Kylie cleared her throat. "A producer from Cuisine TV came in yesterday."

The detective waited for her to continue and finally said, "And what was this producer's name?"

Kylie wet her lips nervously, not wanting to give away too much information. But if someone else's life was possibly in danger, then how could she hold back? "His name is Arnold Stephens. He's doing some TV specials from this area."

"Did you speak with him?"

Nate stepped toward Kylie. "He was interested in possibly filming here."

"That sounds like a great opportunity for your restaurant, Nate. What did you say?" The detective's eyes seemed friendly, but equally as perceptive, as if he soaked in every detail.

Nate shifted his weight. "We said no. The timing's just not good right now."

Kylie could tell that Nate was trying to protect her by not giving away too much of her reason for being here. Still, Kylie couldn't help but think about Suzy. Not that she could imagine that Suzy's disappearance and her stalker had a connection, but still . . . stranger things had happened. Kylie couldn't remain silent.

Kylie sucked in a breath, wishing her heart would stop beating so fast. "May I tell you something that requires a bit of privacy, Detective?"

He stared at her a moment before nodding and lowering his pad of paper. "Okay, Ms. Summers."

Nate nodded toward his office. "Why don't you go back there? I can handle things out here."

The detective followed her into the back, away from the listening ears of customers. Kylie rubbed her hands together, emotions battling inside until finally fear won and rose up to the surface. She tried to swallow it back.

"Detective, I came to Yorktown to get away from a stalker who's been terrorizing me for the last several months. The police back in Lexington, Kentucky, set up a sting that was supposed to take place today to catch the guy, but the officer who was supposed to be my double hurt herself, so the operation has been delayed."

"A stalker, you say?"

"Yes, I have my own cooking show back in Kentucky and the police think my stalker is one of the show's fans." Kylie's head felt woozy, so she sat in Nate's chair. "I didn't want to tell you this out there because I'm trying to stay as low-key as possible while I'm here in Yorktown. That producer, unfortunately, recognized me and wanted to film this week. I'm not comfortable filming until I know this man who's been causing me nightmares is behind bars."

"I don't see any reason why I'd have to share any of this information with anyone, Ms. Summers. I would, however, like the name and number of your contact with the police department back in Kentucky. I'd also like Mr. Stephens's contact information, if you have it."

"I appreciate your discretion," Kylie said. "My brother is the police officer who's been handling much of what's going on. I'd be more than happy to give you his information."

She reached in her pocket and pulled out Mr. Stephens's card. "Here's the producer's information."

"You said that Suzy didn't have any interaction with this producer who came in?"

Kylie shook her head. "None that I know of. But just in case there's any connection, I wanted to let you know the situation I'm in. Only two people know that I'm here—three if you include Arnold Stephens."

"Thank you for sharing."

He turned to leave when Kylie called his name. He paused and looked at her. "Yes?"

"Is there anything I can do to help? I hate feeling so helpless."

"Just keep an eye out for anyone suspicious. And if you think of anything else, let us know."

13

Two hours later, the last table was wiped, the last dish put into the washer and Harvey had headed home for the evening. Kylie leaned with her palms against the counter, dreaming about melting into bed and giving rest to her weary limbs and mind. What a day.

Behind her, Kylie sensed Nate approaching. Maybe it was the whiff of his musky cologne mixed with the scent of cheese, fresh veggies and garlic that gave him away. Would anyone else but a cook enjoy that combination?

Kylie turned and saw him leaning against the counter opposite her with a wry grin on his face. For some reason, the image made her heart race.

She swallowed and dug her nails into the

counter behind her. "We survived."

His eyes looked smoky and intense and captivating all at once. "I'm supposed to be helping you, but I think I got the better end of the deal."

Kylie's cheeks flushed. "I don't know about that."

He pushed himself away from the counter and stepped closer. "You okay? I know today's been stressful for you."

Kylie suddenly felt the need to fan her warm cheeks. "Yeah, I'm okay. Better than Suzy."

Her tone sobered at the mention of Suzy's name.

Nate stood in front of her now, close enough to touch.

That's exactly all she could think about doing. "There's still a chance she could be with a friend somewhere."

Kylie studied his face, the tight lines around his eyes and mouth. "You don't really think that though, do you?"

Nate pressed his lips together as if in thought, then shook his head. "No, not really. But I'm praying the explanation is more along those lines than the other places my mind goes."

"That's probably a good idea."

Nate tilted his head toward her and sucked in a breath before slowly exhaling. "Listen, what do you think about going to catch a late movie? Get away from here for a little while and do something to take your mind off of everything?"

"You might have a very sleepy employee tomorrow." The idea sounded tempting now—very tempting—but she'd regret staying up late when the morning hit. Still, the thought of being swept away by a movie had its allure. Otherwise Kylie would be in her apartment all evening, trying to sleep but unable to because of thoughts of Suzy and her stalker.

Nate's blue eyes glimmered down at her, making her throat dry. "I think I could forgive a sleepy employee, especially when she's such a hardworking employee."

She sucked in a breath, trying to gain composure. Why was Nate having this effect on her? Even when she'd dated Colin she didn't remember feeling this infatuated.

Get a grip, Kylie. "A movie would be a great distraction."

With a promise to meet in ten minutes, Kylie rushed upstairs, wishing she had time to take a shower and get the smell of food off of her. Instead, she settled for clean jeans and her favorite sweater.

Nate was waiting for her downstairs. He smiled

when he spotted her, and Kylie appreciated his effort
to keep her mind off Suzy. Kylie knew that was the
only reason he'd offered to take her to the movies at
this hour. The gesture was sweet, though, for a
moment, she wished there was more to it.

"You ready?" Nate asked as she joined him.

She nodded. Nate took her elbow and led her
outside. The chilly nighttime air cooled her skin,
which seemed to be constantly heating up this
evening. The fresh smell of the river drifted with the
wind, and somewhere in the distance a man played
the guitar and sang.

Kylie hadn't been outside in more days than she
cared to admit. She needed to start remedying that.
Fresh air could do wonders for the mind and body.

After Nate helped her into his truck, they started
down the road. The nighttime sky sparkled around
them as they traveled down the historic Colonial
Parkway. With no lights on the street, the stars
looked clear and vivid. Even the treetops looked
crisper against the black of the sky.

"It's beautiful." Kylie said, gazing out the
window.

"Yeah, I love this road. You'd never know civiliza-
tion is so close."

She glanced at Nate. "You like it here in Yorktown, don't you?"

He shrugged then nodded. "Yeah, I do like it. Most of the time, at least. I've always thought it would be a great place to raise a family. The town has so much history, the locals are great, the tourists are always interesting and the location is right on the water, which is a prerequisite for any place I live."

"Do you boat?" It made sense, Kylie thought. He was former Coast Guard.

"I like to, but I don't have a chance very often. The restaurant keeps me busy. Too busy, probably."

"You ever thought about hiring more staff and giving yourself another day off?"

"I wish I could, but I can't. Not now." Lines formed at his eyes as the words left his mouth.

Kylie nodded and pressed her lips together. She wanted to admonish him that if he didn't hire more staff, he wouldn't have a restaurant to run. She could survive working twelve-hour days for the brief time she was here, but most people wanted a life outside of work. He really needed to take that into consideration after she returned to Kentucky.

She glanced over at Nate and saw that the lines still remained around his eyes, and as he focused on the road, Kylie had a feeling his mind was elsewhere. Probably on the restaurant and his struggles there.

A few minutes later, they pulled into the packed parking lot of the theater. Nate, with his hand on her back, guided her toward the entrance. Just having him close made Kylie feel safe and protected— something she hadn't felt in a long time.

Don't get used to the idea. You'll be leaving soon.

Besides, Nate seemed to think of her as either a little sister or a damsel in distress. Neither was grounds for developing a relationship. Her heart sank at the thought. Why did she wish that a relationship between the two of them was a possibility?

"What do you think?" Nate looked up at the theater marquee, its light softening his features. "Comedy, mystery, sci-fi?"

She glanced up at the titles. "Definitely the comedy." Laughing just might be the perfect medicine.

Inside the theater, sitting beside Nate, Kylie reminded herself that they weren't on a date. But when their elbows brushed, or they both reached for popcorn at the same time, or they laughed together at a punchline, Kylie felt like they'd done this a million times before.

Kylie couldn't even begin to fantasize about what it would be like to date Nate. That was just one big, bad idea. He seemed to like rescuing people, and

Kylie hated to be rescued, so the two would make a terrible pair.

But if they'd make such a terrible pair, why did Kylie enjoy being with him so much?

As they bounced down the road back to Yorktown, Nate thought the movie had worked well as a distraction. Yes, they'd both be tired tomorrow. But getting his mind and Kylie's off of Suzy and the stalker and even the restaurant had been nice.

Kylie stared out the window until, gradually, her head leaned against it and her eyes closed. From her soft breathing, Nate guessed she'd fallen asleep. He had the urge to offer his shoulder or to put his coat over her, but he didn't.

He couldn't get into a relationship with Kylie. She'd be leaving soon. Her situation in being here— more than her personality itself—reminded him too much of Deanna. He couldn't fall for someone like Deanna again. He didn't need to nurse another broken heart when she left, nor did he want to be taken for a fool.

Nate stole a glance at Kylie while she slept. She really was lovely with her soft features and beautifully sculptured face. It seemed like she'd been a part of his life for much longer than a week.

A part of his life? Was she really a part of his life? He stared at the road ahead of him in thought.

The two had been thrown together in unusual circumstances, so of course they'd bonded. His job was to watch over her, to stand guard until her stalker was behind bars. And that's exactly what he intended to do until the man behind the threats against her was behind bars. Nothing more. Nothing less.

He pulled into the parking lot and cut the engine. Silence filled the truck. He glanced over at Kylie as the streetlight bathed her face in a warm yellow. Her breathing sounded so soft and peaceful. He hated to wake her.

As gently as possible, he touched her shoulder. She startled, sitting up ramrod straight. Her eyes darted around in an almost panicked way before settling on Nate. Some of the tension melted from her face as she leaned back into the seat.

"I didn't mean to scare you."

She shook her head. "I can't believe I fell into such a deep sleep. The hum of the truck must have knocked me out."

"Glad you could rest a bit." He nodded toward

the restaurant, which looked a little eerie at this time of the evening with all its lights out. "We better get inside, though. It's late."

She rubbed her eyes. "Thanks again for the movie, Nate. It was good to have a bit of fun in the midst of all of this craziness."

"I agree."

She looked into the distance and frowned. "I hope Suzy's okay."

Nate grabbed her hand and squeezed it, reveling in the softness of her fingers. "The police are working on it."

She squeezed his hand in return, still looking across the parking lot. "Nate, do you think . . ."

He knew exactly where her thoughts were going. "Do I think Suzy's disappearance is linked to your stalker?"

Kylie turned her big eyes back on him, nibbling her lip as she nodded.

"It's doubtful, Kylie, but we can't rule anything out."

Kylie's eyes seemed to search his for answers, for comfort. He wanted to tell her that everything would be okay, but that was a promise he couldn't make yet. Instead, Nate thought about reaching over and touching her cheek, peppering her eyelids with kisses until all of her worry disappeared.

Kylie looked away and offered what appeared to be a forced smile. "I guess we should get inside. We have another busy day ahead of us."

They climbed out of the truck and Nate placed a protective arm around her as they walked toward the back entrance to The Revolutionary Grill. All of the normal town sounds— tourists, fife and drum, kids on the beach—were silenced at this hour. The only sound was that of their footsteps tapping on the pavement.

Just as they reached the door, a crash sounded in the alley.

Kylie clutched at his shirt. Her heart hammered against his arm.

His gaze darted around them, but he didn't see anything. The sound hadn't materialized out of nowhere.

"Get inside. I'll check out the noise." He pushed Kylie behind him.

As he stuck his key into the lock, the clatter sounded again. Nate jerked his head to the left as a figure stepped from the shadows. He braced himself, ready to protect Kylie no matter the cost.

ylie squelched a scream as the man approached. Was this it, the way everything would play out? Was this what had happened to Suzy last night? Had Kylie's stalker found her here? Her heart seemed to pound out of her chest as fear paralyzed the rest of her.

"Go inside, Kylie." Nate's tone left no room for argument.

Kylie's eyes remained glued to the figure approaching them. She held her breath, waiting to see who it was, yet not wanting to see.

"Now, Kylie." Nate's voice was close to a growl. He never took his eyes off the man, and his whole body seemed tight with adrenaline.

Her eyes still on the man, she fumbled with the

doorknob. Her heart pounded an erratic rhythm. Finally, she got enough traction to open the door and back inside.

She vaguely had the thought to call the police, yet she couldn't seem to leave the door, to stop watching whatever would unfold. The man continued to approach Nate, who had bristled like an angry dog. His hands went to his hips and his legs were planted like unmovable trees.

"What do you want?" Nate asked, and Kylie could easily imagine him on duty with the Coast Guard, taking charge of whatever life-or-death situation he faced. She could see where others would bow to his stance and demeanor.

The man took another step forward, his figure a bit hunched and slow. A light from the parking lot caught half of his face.

It couldn't be . . .

It was Frank Watters, town bum. Kylie closed her eyes, feeling both relief and irritation.

Nate retained his stance. "Frank? What are you doing?"

The man shrugged. "Looking for something to eat. Knocked down those trash cans by accident. Have any leftovers you can share?"

Nate shook his head, clearly irritated. "Frank,

you shouldn't be creeping around here at this hour. You should head home before I call the police. This is my property and you're trespassing."

Frank laughed, a pathetic sound that showed a variety of missing teeth. "No one appreciates me snooping through their trash cans during the day either, you see."

"Were you out here last night also, Frank?" Nate asked. "Were you here when Suzy left and started toward her car?"

Kylie knew what he was getting at with the question. Had he seen Suzy? Worse yet, had he done something to Suzy? Kylie didn't know enough about the man to know if he was unstable, unlucky or both. At this moment, she wasn't sure she wanted to find out. In fact, she preferred that Nate would just come in and get away from the man also. Frank's eyes had a wild look about them, one that made Kylie nervous.

"I don't remember last night. I barely remember today. What is it? Wednesday?" The man let out a cackling laugh. "And who's Suzy?"

He was drunk, Kylie realized.

From where Kylie stood, she could see Nate's jaw muscle flex and his eyes narrow. "Frank, go home. Now."

Frank held his hands in the air, his battered jacket dwarfing his thin body. "I'm not bothering anyone. And you throw out so much good food."

"If you need something to eat, you can just ask me, Frank. You don't have to go through the trash."

Frank straightened. "Okay then, I need something to eat."

Kylie watched Nate, waiting for his response. Don't let the man inside here, she begged silently. Don't let him in.

Nate paused a moment before nodding toward the restaurant. "Come inside. I'll fix you something." He opened the door and stepped in.

Kylie grabbed his arm before Frank could enter and lowered her voice. "Nate, I don't think this is a good idea. What if he . . .?"

"Feeding him can't hurt anything," he whispered. "Why don't you go upstairs to your room. Lock your door. I'll be okay, but I'd feel better if you stayed away from Frank right now. He's never any fun when he's drunk."

"I don't like this, Nate. I'm not going to be able to sleep knowing you're down here with him. What about Suzy?"

"I'll see if I can find anything out, okay? Now

don't worry about me." He leaned in and kissed her forehead.

Kylie's cheeks flushed. The action had seemed so natural, like he'd done it a million times before.

Nate grasped the sides of her arms and bent down to look her square in the eye. "Go ahead upstairs."

Kylie nodded and started up the stairs, just as she heard Frank step into the building and mutter a string of expletives.

Nate hadn't intended to kiss Kylie's forehead, but her concern over his safety had gotten the best of him. What surprised him even more was how easily the action had come and how much he wanted to do it more often.

When he'd thought she might be in danger, he'd felt a rush of protection . . . and affection.

He put Kylie and his unexpected kiss out of his mind for the moment. Right now, he had to feed Frank and send him home. Certainly if the man was hungry, he had no problem offering him food. As a Christian, it was the least he could do. In fact, he was commanded to do it. There was a line between being compassionate and being cautious, however. He'd never encourage Kylie to let the man into her apartment alone, but Nate knew he could handle himself.

Frank followed him into the kitchen, smelling like he hadn't taken a bath in weeks.

"What are you in the mood for, Frank? A sandwich maybe?"

"One of those corned beef ones you guys serve would be nice."

"One Cornwallis Corned Beef coming up." Nate began pulling out everything he needed while Frank made himself comfortable at the small table set up in the back for employees.

"So, do you hang out around here a lot at night, Frank?" Nate sliced another piece of corned beef.

"Depends on what I'm in the mood to eat. People are so wasteful."

Nate sliced the rustic bread and slathered on some sauce. "You don't have to eat trash, Frank. I know there are plenty of people who would feed you."

He shrugged. "Don't want to be a bother."

Nate closed the bread together, put it on a plate and placed the sandwich in front of Frank. His eyes lit up and he grabbed the food.

"It's not a bother, Frank," Nate said. "What can I

get you to drink?"

He asked for a soda, and as Nate went to grab a cup, he pondered how to find out more information about whether or not Frank had seen Suzy. If the man were sober, he'd be much easier to talk to.

He brought the still fizzing drink over to Frank and, as he sat down at the table, pushed the cup toward him. "Did you see Suzy last night, Frank?"

He paused from eating only long enough to say, "I told you. I don't know a Suzy."

"Certainly you remember Suzy, Frank. She's young, pretty. Has short dark hair on the bottom, bright red hair on top. Very friendly. You've always had an eye for pretty girls."

Frank nodded toward the back door, a glob of sauce at the corner of his lip that he either didn't notice or didn't care about. "That new girl you have working here is easy on the eyes."

Nate's hackles rose at the mention of Kylie. *Remain calm and keep cool.* "Yes, she is. She's a great help around here."

"She goes pale mighty easily, though." He nodded with certainty, like he'd seen it happen many times.

"What do you mean?"

"She's jumpy."

"How do you know that, Frank?"

"I like to sit on the beach and watch people. You know that." Again, he nodded toward the stairway. "That girl you hired always looks scared, like she's worried someone's following her."

If Nate wasn't certain that Frank had been in Virginia for the past several weeks and had no means of transportation, he would worry that he might be Kylie's stalker. But that just wasn't possible. Still, he'd stay on guard, just to be on the safe side.

Most of the time, Frank wasn't a menace; he simply hung around town at inopportune times. Tourists had even complained about him. But still, no one could truly help Frank until he was ready to help himself.

A hand of guidance had been offered to him many times before, but he'd refused it. Frank very easily could be the town's best resource on what was going on and where, if he didn't drink and if he could remember things a little better. Frank always seemed to be watching and observing, even trying once to blackmail someone and serving a six-month sentence for extortion as a result.

But certainly if he could remember that Kylie went pale and looked frightened, he would remember Suzy.

"Don't tell me you can remember that about one of my new employees but not remember Suzy at all. That doesn't add up, Frank."

"I dunno anything about that girl! I told you already!" The man's voice rose until he began coughing. He reached into his pocket and pulled out a scarf to cover his mouth.

Nate paused halfway to the sink and stared at it.

It was the same purple scarf that Suzy had worn around her head yesterday before she disappeared.

Nate closed his eyes. *Dear Lord, what had Frank done to Suzy?*

15

Kylie tried to sleep, but finally gave up. Her mind played out several scenarios of what might be going on downstairs, none of them ending well. One involved Frank pulling out a hidden gun. Certainly she'd hear gunfire if that happened. Another image was of Frank pulling a knife on Nate as he fixed a meal for the man.

Was Nate okay? Was Frank truly harmless or was he a predator?

Kylie threw the covers off of her and began pacing the length of her apartment. She'd promised Nate she'd stay up here. But when the restaurant's back door opened and voices carried up the stairs, her curiosity peaked. She hurried to the window and spotted a sheriff's car outside.

Alarms sounded in her head. The sheriff? What was going on?

She yanked a sweatshirt over her head, gripped the door handle and charged into the stairwell.

By the back door, the sheriff argued with Frank. Beyond them, Nate stood with his arms crossed, scowling. His expression softened when he spotted her. He dropped his arms to the side as he took the stairs two by two to reach her.

Thank you, Lord, that he's okay.

"What's going on?" She stuffed her hands into her pockets, searching Nate's face for any sign that he was hurt.

Nate stepped close and lowered his voice. "Frank has Suzy's scarf. He claims he didn't see her last night, but . . ."

"Then how did he get her scarf?" Kylie's voice rose in pitch.

"That's what the sheriff is trying to figure out. He's going to take him down to the station for questioning. Why don't you go back into the apartment and I'll let you know when they're gone? Okay?"

Kylie nodded, not wanting to be around Frank right now anyway, especially when she thought about what the man might have done to Suzy. She squeezed Nate's hand and then slipped back inside the apartment and locked the door. She heard Nate running down the steps again and the sound of voices, though she couldn't make out the words.

She leaned against the door, her heart racing. What could Frank have done with Suzy? Was she okay? Being held captive somewhere? Or had Frank done something worse? She shuddered.

She prayed it wasn't too late, that Suzy was okay and safe and just waiting to be found.

Walking toward the window, she glanced outside again and saw the sheriff leading a belligerent Frank into the squad car. She hoped the sheriff truly would get to the bottom of this.

She saw Nate watching the scene from the stoop outside. His hands were planted on his hips and he shook his head as if weary and frustrated. A moment later, he came inside and Kylie heard him climbing the stairs. She went to the door and unlocked it. When she pulled it open, he stood on the other side.

She extended her arm behind her, inviting him in. She wanted to wrap her arms around him and try to relieve some of his weariness. She didn't, though.

"Want some tea?" she offered instead.

He shook his head and sat at the dinette. "No, thanks."

Kylie sat across from him, lacing her fingers together on the table. "What happened? Do they know where Suzy is?"

"Frank still won't admit that he even saw her. I'm hoping the sheriff will be able to get more information from him."

"Is Frank dangerous?"

"He's mostly just a nuisance. I hate to say it that way, but it's true. He won't help himself. Instead, he just makes everyone else miserable. But I really can't see him being violent."

"But Suzy's scarf..."

He rubbed his hands over his face. "I know. Believe me, I know."

"Did you find out anything else?"

He slid his hands down his face and dropped them to his side as he leaned back in the chair. "No, I didn't. I wish I had."

"You did well, Nate. That was really nice of you to offer him some food."

"I should probably do it more often, but when I close the restaurant, I'm usually exhausted. Plus, the idea of Frank hanging around doesn't do much for business. So don't take me for a saint. I struggle just as much as anyone with caring for the 'least of these.'"

"Isn't that what the Christian walk is about? Giving our best. All of us are far from perfect. Thank goodness for the grace of God. I'd be nowhere without it, that's for sure."

"Why do you say it with such a heavy heart?"

Kylie shrugged. "I don't know. Just being in the situation I've been in for the past few months, I guess. I cling to God when times are tough, but when times are good, I seem to think I can do it on my own. It's a lesson I've been constantly trying to conquer for my whole life."

"I think a lot of us are like that."

Her mind drifted back to her teen years. She closed her eyes. "I've never felt closer to God than when I had lymphoma. I felt like I knew God intimately. Then I went into remission. I'm not really sure what happened. My church attendance stopped being what it should. I thought I could love God without immersing myself in His word or gathering with other believers. I thought just believing was enough. But I'm tired of living like this."

"It sounds like you've had some good realizations, Kylie. It all goes back to that grace thing you were talking about earlier."

She nodded. "You're right. Absolutely right."

"How about we pray for Suzy together? Would that be okay?"

"That would be more than okay."

Nate reached across the table and took her hand. Together they bowed their heads and lifted prayers for Suzy's safety, for peace for her family, for justice to whoever had done this to her.

After saying amen, she reluctantly pulled her hands away from Nate's. Kylie felt a special connection with Nate. Praying with others always seemed to do that.

He cleared his throat and glanced at his watch. "I should try to get a few hours of rest."

"Me, too."

Nate's warm eyes settled on hers. "Good night, Kylie."

"Good night, Nate." Kylie smiled, her heart racing more than it probably should.

When she'd met Nate in the parking lot on that stormy night, she would never have thought that in such a short time he'd leave her smiling like a lovesick teenager, but that's exactly what she was doing.

She stood and leaned against the door, remembering the feeling of Nate's hand in hers. She was still smiling as she slipped into bed for the evening.

Seven o'clock came too soon for Kylie. Despite the hectic pace of last evening, she must have fallen into a deep sleep, because when she woke up, she immediately heard voices and machinery outside the building.

She walked to the window facing the river. Water spurted like a fountain from the asphalt and filled the street below. At that moment, crews paused from their noise-making activities to stare at the mess.

Kylie threw on some clothes and hurried downstairs. She rushed through the kitchen and found Nate standing in the dining room, watching everything outside the picture windows. He turned when she walked in.

"What's going on?" She stood beside him.

"Water-main break. I woke up an hour ago and saw the street was flooded. Called the city and now they're staring at the problem, trying to figure out what to do."

Kylie shoved her hands into her jean pockets and

absorbed the information. "What does that mean for business today?"

"It means we have no business today. I'm not about to let customers in through the kitchen, and there's no way they're wading through the water to get to the front door. Plus, we have no water." He wrinkled his lips and glanced her way. "I guess that's a blessing and a curse."

"Maybe there's some other stuff we can do in the kitchen to get ready for opening again on Monday."

He nodded, his gaze fixed on the men outside. "Maybe."

Kylie paused to stare at the city work crew outside for another moment. Finally she turned to Nate, ready to ask the questions that were most on her mind. "Any word on Suzy? Frank?"

He shook his head. "I haven't called yet. I will once I get into my office."

A few minutes later Nate disappeared into his cubbyhole, and Kylie busied herself by cleaning shelves, rearranging plates and throwing away old food from the refrigerator.

Darlene stopped by, as she did every morning, but this time without desserts. "That's quite the mess outside."

Kylie paused and stretched for a moment,

grateful for a break. "Needless to say, we're closed for business."

"That's what I figured. I'm sorry to hear that. I know it's bad for business."

"Speaking of business, how are things at the bed-and-breakfast?"

Darlene's face lit with a smile. "I can't complain. I've had one guest who came Thursday and plans to stay for a week. I told him to come try the restaurant, but he seems preoccupied with some business he's attending to. I also have two couples on weekend getaways and four sisters who decided to explore some American heritage."

Kylie smiled. "That's great."

Kylie knew Darlene and Harvey worried about business, like many people in their position did. Kylie was glad to hear things were going well for them. Before Kylie could ask any more questions, Nate appeared from out of his office. The lines around his eyes looked deeper as he approached. Kylie and Darlene both paused and waited for him to share whatever was on his mind.

"I'm not sure if you heard yet or not, but Frank was in the restaurant last night, and he had the scarf Suzy was wearing when she disappeared. The police have him in custody, but he still claims he knows nothing. He said he found that scarf on the ground the night Suzy disappeared." Nate shook his head. "And there's still no word on Suzy. No one seems to know or to have seen anything. Her parents are beside themselves."

"Is there anything we can do?" Darlene asked.

He shook his head. "The police are still asking questions so they can know where to start looking, even. The best we can do right now is pray."

Kylie nodded. "I've been doing that and will definitely continue."

"Everyone in town has been praying," Darlene added. "We'll find her. I just know we will." She patted Nate's arm and then hugged Kylie. "Let me know if I can do anything."

"I'm sorry the restaurant will be closed today. I have lots of guests I was hoping to send over here."

When Darlene left, Nate shifted his eyes to the crew in front of the store. He stared at them for a moment before running a hand down his face as if to wipe away exhaustion. Then he turned to Kylie. "What do you say we forget about work and go for a walk?"

Kylie put down the silverware she was rolling. "A walk? But what about the restaurant?"

"It can wait." He stretched out his hand. "What do you say?"

Kylie looked at him a moment before smiling. "I say let's do it." She grabbed his hand and he pulled her to her feet.

As she glanced out the window, she saw the fog still hung heavily outside. "I thought this would have rolled out by now."

"Nah, the fog likes to settle here in Yorktown for some reason. Being right here on the water helps. I always say it gives the place atmosphere."

They stepped outside into the damp day. Beyond the building, the sound of crews working on the street filled the air. Kylie pulled her sweatshirt more tightly around her to ward off some of the heavy moisture in the air.

"Weather too bad for you?"

She shook her head. "Are you kidding? It feels great to get outside."

"I thought we could walk over to the National Battlefield. It's pretty interesting there, whether you're a history buff or not."

"Let's go."

As they moved away from the restaurant, walking between historic buildings where treaties were signed and history took place, the sound of the fife and drum drifted through the air. Soon enough, a group of teenagers dressed in Colonial garb appeared, walking in formation. The music lent a magic feel to the surroundings.

Kylie sucked in a breath, cool air filling her lungs. It felt so good to stretch her legs and to be outside. She didn't realize how much she loved being in nature until she was stuck inside all day.

"For a Saturday, this place is pretty dead." Nate glanced around at the barren streets. "We usually have tourist groups throughout the year."

"Maybe you're not losing a lot of business today after all."

He offered a half smile. "Are you always such an optimist?"

Kylie stuffed her hands into her pockets. "No, not always. But I do find it helps me when I can think positively."

They reached a clearing and before them stretched Surrender Field, the place where the war for this country had been won. They wandered the gentle hills and looked at the historic cannons that marked the battlefield.

In the distance stood a cemetery. They walked quietly toward it, side by side, dew glistening on the tops of their shoes and dampening the edges of their pants. Fog still hung heavy around them, making the historic marker feel even more haunted.

In the cemetery, Kylie reflected on the names she read, names of people who had died fighting for this country during the Revolutionary War. She thanked God for the sacrifices made in order to give her freedom. She thanked Him for the ultimate sacrifice that His son made on the cross in order to give her life.

Greater love has no man than this, that he would give up his life for another.

The verse flittered through her mind. Nate's image flashed into her mind. He was the kind of man who'd give up his life to save someone else. He was a good man. Honorable. Men like him were few and far between.

"I love coming here to reflect on life." Nate leaned against a fence at the edge of the cemetery, his hands stuffed into the pockets of his jacket.

"Cemeteries are a great place to put life into perspective, that's for sure."

Kylie averted her gaze to the left at a movement she saw there. Another tourist? She searched the area, but saw no one, just an old house and some headstones and towering trees.

Nate appeared at her side. "What is it?"

Kylie blinked rapidly. "I guess I'm just seeing things."

They began walking between the headstones together. The skin on Kylie's neck prickled. Was someone watching them? She paused and turned. She and Nate were the only ones in the cemetery. Everything that had happened lately was making her paranoid.

Nate's cell phone rang. He pulled it from his belt, checked the number and then glanced back at Kylie. "I've got to take this. Will you excuse me for a moment?"

Kylie nodded and watched as he walked toward one of the towering nearby trees. His voice sounded low and she couldn't make out what the call was about. The water main break, maybe? She continued walking, not straying too far from Nate.

She paused. The feeling of unseen eyes on her was all too familiar. She'd become accustomed to it back in Kentucky. Without turning her head, she scanned the area in front of her. Woods that ended at the river. She saw no one there, not even a wild animal.

Trying to appear casual, she turned toward a nearby cannon, but her eyes wandered over her surroundings. When her gaze reached the visitor center, she stopped. Was that a figure she'd seen dart around the corner? Or were her eyes playing tricks on her?

The place was already foggy, with shifty shadows and low visibility. Perhaps her paranoia was at play again.

"Kylie?"

She let out a small scream and jumped, spinning around toward the voice.

"Whoa, it's just me." Nate stood there with his arms raised.

Kylie's heart rate slowed some. "Nate," she breathed in relief.

"Who did you think it was?"

She shrugged, her gaze darting toward the visitor center again. "I don't know. I just keep feeling like we're not alone here."

Nate scanned the area. "I don't see anyone."

"I know. I don't either. I guess it's more of a feeling. Maybe it's just something that's been ingrained in me after all of my experiences back in Kentucky."

He put an arm to her waist. "We should probably head back, anyway."

"Why? Is everything okay? Was the phone call about Suzy?"

He glanced toward his phone. "The phone call?

No. That was . . . that was nothing. No news yet." He began leading her back toward the road. "Now, let's get you home."

Kylie nodded, but she couldn't help but wonder who the phone call had been from. There was something Nate wasn't telling her. Kylie's heart twisted at the possibility. Had it been Bruce? The sheriff? She sucked in a breath. She would have to trust Nate. If the phone call was something she needed to know about, Nate would tell her . . . wouldn't he?

16

By the time Nate arrived back at the restaurant, his thoughts over the phone call had been replaced by worries over Kylie's safety. Certainly Kylie had imagined things while in the cemetery. Her stalker couldn't have found her here.

Or could he?

Nate twisted his key in the lock with such force that the metal nearly broke. He hoped Kylie didn't notice as he led her inside. He'd remain on guard, make sure Kylie didn't get out of his sight. He wished Bruce would catch the guy behind these threats to Kylie and throw him in jail. He'd feel better once Kylie was safe and this madman was no longer a threat.

Of course, once she was safe, that meant she could go back to Kentucky. Why did that realization cause his gut to twist?

Could it be because Kylie had been the only bright spot about the restaurant for the past week? His heart lurched at the thought.

"Well, I'm at your disposal. Anything you need me to do?" Kylie stood staring at him, looking so earnest with her doe-like eyes, tiny chin and steady gaze.

He wanted to touch that adorable chin, to see if her skin felt as soft as he imagined. He kept his arms at his sides, however. "Why don't you take the rest of the day off and I'll get caught up on my paperwork. I've been working you too hard anyway."

Kylie remained where she stood and shrugged. "I actually prefer to stay busy. It keeps my mind off of things."

"Okay, then." He nodded, wishing the weather was a little nicer today so they could remain outside with reasonable visibility. The fog made it too easy for someone to conceal themselves, and Nate couldn't chance that. "How about if you fix us lunch?"

She nodded, looking pleased as her gaze traveled to the kitchen. "I can do that. Any requests?"

"Whatever your specialty is. Just remember, you'll have to use some of the extra water jugs I have stored in the pantry. The water line still hasn't been turned on."

"No problem." She glanced toward the dining area and beyond, to where it appeared the beach had expanded to reach the restaurant. "I wonder how long it will take the crews to fix all of this? What a mess."

"I'm going to go talk to them in a minute, see if there are any updates." He stepped away, his heart thumping uncontrollably. He liked being near Kylie. Probably too much. Which meant he needed some space before his heart got him into trouble. "Do you need anything?"

"Nope. Not a thing."

Nate walked into the dining area and opened the front door. Water, probably a foot high, still stood on the street. Thankfully it stopped right before it reached the stoop of his restaurant and remained outside. The last thing he needed was the inside of his restaurant flooded.

At least the gushing from underground had stopped, he reasoned. That had to mean some progress was being made. The city crew had a machine drilling into the asphalt. The supervisor walked toward Nate when he stepped outside.

"So, what's the update?" Nate had to shout to be heard over the machinery.

"Water should be back on in a few hours. This street will be closed at least until Monday, though. Those pipes down there are old. It's gonna take some time to get them replaced properly. Probably should have been replaced years ago. We're working as fast as we can to resolve the situation, sir."

Nate nodded, then made his way back inside. Kylie whipped up something in a metal bowl as he passed. He tried to pinpoint the mouthwatering scents swirling around him . . . garlic, parsley, Kylie's sweet perfume?

He shook the thought away and went to his office. He had to look at his books one more time. At his desk, he pulled them out and settled them on top of his desk calendar. The numbers blurred together. He rubbed his eyes.

Focus, Nate. Focus.

He did a few calculations and ran some numbers before sighing again. He wasn't seeing things. A weight that felt heavier than rescuing a wet, three-hundred pound man from the ocean pressed on him.

At this rate, he'd be bankrupt by next year.

He put his hand on his throbbing forehead. Why had this situation turned into such a nightmare? He'd hoped being in the restaurant would make him fall in love with it. Instead, the opposite had happened. He only disliked it here more and more every day.

His only hope seemed to be the man who'd called him today, interested in potentially buying the place. But was Nate really ready to sell?

A picture of his father on the shelf above his desk stared down at him. He kept the photo there to remind him of how much his dad had loved this place. Seeing it reminded him of the sacrifices his father had made in order to give him a good life.

Wasn't that what love was about? Sacrifice? Isn't that why he kept this place open, even though working here made him miserable?

Kylie drifted into his mind. What she would say if she knew he was talking to a buyer? She seemed so loyal to her family and to her values. She'd probably never understand why he was tempted to sell.

Little did she realize that Nate had no desire for wealth or status or even a trophy wife, for that matter.

That was probably why Deanna had left him.

She'd wanted Nate to be someone he wasn't. Why hadn't he seen that earlier?

He knew one thing—he'd never fall into that trap again. Her whining, her constant mini-emergencies that were anything but emergencies, her insecurity. Sometimes it took a bad relationship to make you realize what you wanted in a good relationship.

He needed someone strong and independent, who didn't care about worldly things as much as she cared about the heart.

Kylie stuck her head into the doorway, the worry from earlier today gone from her eyes and replaced with lightness. "Hey, Boss Man, it's time for lunch."

He stood, closing the books before Kylie caught a glimpse of what a mess the restaurant was really in. "It smells great." He stretched. "And you don't have to call me Boss Man. In fact, please don't."

She smiled. "Got it. And I'm glad it smells good. I made one of my favorite dishes. All my viewers seemed to really like it also, which makes it even more satisfying to me."

He followed her to a table in the dining area that was elegantly set for two. He pulled a chair out for her, feeling a bit as if they were on a date. She gingerly sat and he lowered himself across from her.

Before him was a large bowl of pasta and a colorful salad.

He looked at the artfully arranged food. "Now, what exactly is this?"

"I call it Salmon in a Net." She smiled. "It's just some blackened salmon with linguine in a lemon butter sauce. The salad is called Florida Fields. It has cranberries, walnuts and a few other secret ingredients."

Everything smelled delicious. After praying, he dug in. The food truly was good. Really good. Everything tasted fresh and hit different parts of his taste buds. Kylie watched him a moment.

"You like it?" Kylie chewed on her lip in what appeared to be anxious anticipation. Did she really care what he thought of her dish? Delight rushed through him at the possibility. "Like it? I love it."

She smiled—beamed, actually—and then picked up her fork to eat. A moment later she cleared her throat. A serious expression stretched across her face, one that it appeared she tried to conceal but did a poor job of. "So Nate, have you ever considered trying out a few new recipes here? Your menu has been the same for quite some time, from what I hear."

Nate swallowed his food and wiped his mouth as

he absorbed her question. "New recipes? What's wrong with the ones we have?"

People—his regulars—came into the restaurant because they had favorite dishes they liked to order time and time again.

Kylie tilted her head. "What's wrong with them? Nothing, I suppose, but—"

"Why fix what's not broken, then?"

She paused a moment, as if in thought. "May I speak openly for a moment, Nate?"

"Please do."

"I think you could do so much more with this restaurant, Nate," she said.

He offered a slight nod. "Go on."

"The crab cakes you serve, for instance—they're frozen. Do you realize how much better they would taste if they were fresh? It wouldn't be that much more work and it could make a huge difference. And you get your fish from a wholesale club. You should buy them fresh, utilize some of the local fishermen who get their catfish from the river right here in front of the restaurant." She pointed toward the windows. "Or how about the outside of the place? I bet patrons would love it if you set up some cafe tables with little umbrellas. They would eat here just so they could sit outside and enjoy the view."

Just listening to her suggestions somehow made Nate feel weary. "All of those ideas might work in an ideal situation, but this is not an ideal situation. There are other things at play with running this restaurant that you don't understand, Kylie. I'm barely hanging on here. You have no idea."

Her hopeful expression fell slightly and she drew in a deep breath. "I just think you could go from barely hanging on to being a great success. I'm not an expert, but I am passionate about food and about restaurants. And this place could be so much more. You need more staff. You need staff that care. You need to give up some of your responsibility—"

He shook his head trying in vain to hide his frustration. "I can barely afford the staff I have. I don't think you have any idea what's it's like when I have to do payroll every week and I go in the red, or when I have to pay the bills for the restaurant out of my savings." He paused, his gaze set on her. "I like the restaurant. I really do. But it just isn't working. This just isn't working. And it never will."

Kylie dropped her hands. Was he talking about the restaurant or her? Either way, it was clear that she had no place here. She had to keep her distance—from the restaurant and Nate.

She stood from the table and placed her napkin beside her plate. "I'll be out of your hair soon. I'm sorry my being here has been a headache to you." She hurried toward the kitchen, grabbed a dish towel and began wiping down the counter.

"That's not what I meant, Kylie."

She whirled around. "That's exactly what you meant, Nate. And that's okay. I don't like having people do favors for me. I prefer to get by on my own two feet. So it seems we're both out of our comfort zone."

She started to turn and continue cleaning, but Nate grabbed her arm.

"I'm sorry, Kylie. Sometimes being out of your comfort zone is a good thing. And you do have a lot of good ideas. I've just . . ." He shook his head and looked around the kitchen, feeling like a foreigner in the very place he owned.

"Given up?"

His eyes met her soft, compassionate ones. "Yeah, I guess that's right. I'm tired of trying, yet I'm too stubborn to give up."

Kylie stepped closer, putting her hurt feelings to

the side. "Nate, this isn't your passion. You never wanted to be a restaurant owner or cook or business-man, even. You should sell. I think that's what your dad would want you to do."

"You didn't even know my father, Kylie."

She touched his arm. "But Harvey and Darlene have told me that he was just like you. And I know you. I know if you had a son, you'd want him to be happy. I can't imagine your father would want you to be miserable just to keep his dream alive."

At her proclamation, the tension drained from his shoulders. His head dropped toward the floor and his hands went to his hips. When he pulled his head up, Kylie's eyes met his. She tried to read the emotion there. Relief? Gratitude?

"You really believe that?"

She reached up and touched the stubble on his chin. "I do." She lowered her hand until it rested on his chest.

Nate's fingers trailed across her cheek, his touch sending electricity through her. Kylie's heart seemed to simultaneously speed up and freeze at the same time. She couldn't tear her eyes away from Nate's.

He looked at her lips. Then back up to her eyes. His thumb caressed her cheek.

Kylie sucked in a breath and closed her eyes. The next instant, his lips covered hers. Soft, gentle but firm. His arms circled her waist, pulling her closer. Kylie melted into the moment, enjoying the feeling of being held and protected and safe.

As soon as the kiss began, it ended.

Nate pulled away and pressed his forehead against hers, as if his emotions tortured him. Kylie could feel his heart racing underneath her hand, which still rested on his chest.

"I probably shouldn't have done that," he mumbled.

Kylie's head was spinning around equally as fast as Nate's heart raced. "Me, neither."

Despite her words, she couldn't seem to step back from him. Something unseen kept her grounded where she was—in his arms. Her brain told her this was a bad idea. That Nate would tell her what to do, have too much say so in her life. Hadn't she been there before? Her relationship with Colin had turned out to be a disaster. So why was she standing here now?

"We're a bad idea, aren't we?" she whispered.

He pulled his head back just far enough to stare into her eyes. "Probably. But there's just something about you, Kylie Summers . . . you capture my heart whenever you're with me.

"I'm going to be going back to Kentucky soon . . ." She wanted to say that she would give up her life there to be here with him. But she didn't. She had to keep her independence. She couldn't fall into the same traps she had before.

Nate closed his eyes again. "I know." He kissed her forehead and then pulled her into a hug. "I'm as anxious as you are for this stalker to be caught, but . . ."

He didn't have to finish. Kylie knew that he didn't want her to go back to Kentucky, either. She'd never dreamed when she came here that she'd develop these feelings for Nate so quickly.

She stepped back and swiped her hair behind her shoulders, keeping her eyes on Nate's chest. "We should pretend that never happened."

She looked up in time to see confusion flash in Nate's eyes until finally he stepped back also. "You're probably right. It would be the best thing to do."

Why did she feel disappointed that Nate agreed with her? Sometimes she didn't make sense to herself. "I think I will take the rest of the day off, if that's okay with you. I'm feeling exhausted."

He nodded stiffly. "Of course. You deserve the

time off. I'll meet you downstairs for church tomorrow, if you'd like a ride."

"Thanks." She hurried upstairs and closed the door to her apartment, wishing those locks would make her heart feel equally as safe as her person.

*N*ate walked back to his office, leaving lunch on the table to be cleaned up later.

What had he been thinking? One minute Kylie had infuriated him and the next moment he was kissing her.

He rubbed his temples. He couldn't deny that he was attracted to Kylie. He'd been attracted to her from the moment he set eyes on her delicate figure and had seen those beautiful brown eyes.

But was she just like Deanna? Would she waltz in, using him until another opportunity came along, and then waltz out when he was no longer useful? Kylie wasn't like Deanna, he told himself for the millionth time. Kylie had her own cooking show back in Kentucky. She had opinions on how to make his restaurant better, knowing that she had nothing to gain from the restaurant either changing or remaining as it was. She simply offered her suggestions as a way of trying to help Nate.

He had to admit she had some good ideas. If he had the energy, he might try to make some improvements. But Kylie was right—Nate had simply given up on the place. He needed to remedy that.

When Kylie told him he should sell . . . it felt like a burden had been lifted from him. He wasn't sure why he wanted her approval or why it meant so much to him. But it did.

Her words, for him, had sealed the attraction between them.

Still, she was a woman on the run. Vulnerable. In a precarious situation. He needed to give her space.

He rubbed his eyes again. Yes, it was best that they weren't spending time together right now. But if he were honest with himself, he'd admit that he'd rather be with Kylie right now than doing anything else.

Kylie's heart raced a few extra beats the next

morning when she saw Nate standing at the bottom of the stairs wearing khaki pants and a crisp striped button-down shirt. He was so handsome. His hair naturally seemed to spike up before flopping in a haphazard manner. He always sported the slight shadow of a beard, and his physique was lean and trim.

She looked away before he spotted her admiring him.

She'd spent a miserable evening trying to not think about him or their kiss. But she'd been unsuccessful as the moment replayed in her head over and over again. As she approached, she glanced up long enough to acknowledge him.

Nate offered a small smile when he spotted her. He stuffed his hands deep into his pockets and averted his gaze also. He obviously regretted what had happened yesterday, too. They'd both simply given in to the moment. A big mistake.

"Hey, you," Nate mumbled.

Kylie sucked in a breath, not prepared for the fact that hearing his voice would cause her heart to race. "Morning."

"I'm glad you're joining me again at church this morning. Darlene and Harvey will be happy to see you."

At least someone will be happy to have me there.

As Nate opened the door, Kylie wanted to slip her hand into the crook of his arm, but she stopped herself. She needed to take some steps back. It didn't help that every part of her seemed to be pulled to Nate like a magnet. They stepped outside, and sunlight greeted them. Even the wind seemed to be cooperating today, feeling balmy instead of chilly.

After a silent ride to church, they finally found a seat in the sanctuary. When Nate slipped his arm around the back of the pew, Kylie reasoned that it was out of comfort. And when she scooted closer to him, she told herself it was only because a family had slid into the pew beside them. Deep inside, she had to admit that she felt safe and protected next to Nate. The feeling was one she wanted to cling to, especially with everything that had happened over the past several months. Feeling safe was something that was hard to come by.

How would she feel when she went back to Kentucky? Her stalker would be behind bars by then. But still, she couldn't imagine feeling protected anywhere without Nate by her side. What did their future hold, though?

Nate had probably concluded that a relationship between the two could never work, just as Kylie had.

Soon Kylie would be going back to Kentucky. She'd resume life there and Nate would resume life here.

The thought was heavy on her mind for the rest of the church service.

With Kylie securely in his truck after church, he turned to her. "Listen, it's a nice day outside. I need to do something to relieve some stress. What do you think about taking a bike ride down the Colonial Parkway?"

"I'd love it." Anything beat staying in her apartment with only her thoughts for company.

Nate borrowed the bikes from Darlene and Harvey. They were old-style beach cruisers, but Kylie welcomed the larger seats and more relaxed ride. While Nate got the bikes, Kylie made them a lunch and packed it into a backpack.

Outside, dressed in a sweatshirt and jeans, Kyle felt the sun warm her shoulders and a balmy breeze ruffle her hair. Spring was right around the corner, and Kylie welcomed the change of weather—not only physically, but emotionally also. Her heart had been in winter mode for way too long now.

Nate pointed out various landmarks as they pedaled. Their steady rhythm almost made it seem as if nothing had transpired between them yesterday. Almost.

A good number of other people had the same idea as Nate and Kylie. Large groups of teens rode together. A few people who seemed to be training for a race bolted past them, doggedly focused. Families with children on bike seats or on tricycles leisurely pedaled beside the river.

Kylie could get used to weekends like this, she thought.

They biked for an hour and a half before they found a grassy embankment to pull over at and have their picnic. Kylie welcomed the change of pace as she stretched her legs and shook out a blanket. Soon they settled on the quilt with sandwiches, fruit and bottled water between them.

Kylie almost dreaded this time, because it meant conversation. Throughout the day, other things or people had distracted them from discussing anything other than church, the weather and the water main break. Even the restaurant seemed to be a taboo subject right now. So just what would they talk about?

Nate cleared his throat. "Listen, Kylie, I'm sorry that I didn't listen to your ideas about the restaurant when you shared them."

"I'm sorry I threw them on you."

He smiled. "You didn't throw them on me. I just

tend to get overwhelmed whenever I think about the restaurant. I'm trying to do the right thing by everyone—"

"Including your dad."

He glanced up and nodded. "Yes, including my dad. I just don't know how much longer I can keep it up."

Kylie reached over and squeezed his hand. "You'll make the right decision, Nate. I know the restaurant means a lot to you."

"I wish I had the same confidence about the place." Nate shook his head and straightened his back. "Let's talk about something different. I meant to tell you earlier that I talked to your brother last night."

Kylie paused with her sandwich midair. "Did you?"

"The sting has been rescheduled for this Tuesday."

She frowned. Why hadn't her brother called her himself to share the news? Was this just another way he was trying to baby her?

"Why didn't he tell me?" She pouted. "I don't like it when people treat me like I'm fragile. I'm stronger than people think."

"Life is about being interdependent on people. None of us can truly stand on our own two feet."

"My family still treats me like a child. It's like I'm frozen in time at the age I was diagnosed with lymphoma. They'll never see me as an adult."

"You got all of that because your brother called me instead of you?"

"It's been going on for as long as I remember, Nate. Strangely enough, I seem to be drawn to people who like to baby me. I guess I fall back on what I know." Kylie thought about Colin, about how easily she'd slipped into that bad relationship. Of course, Colin had been worse than her family. He'd tried to control everything in her life, he'd belittled her and made her feel incompetent, as if she screwed up everything on her own.

"Your brother tried to reach you, but your cell phone was off. He called me instead."

Kylie looked at the blanket, suddenly feeling foolish.

"Kylie, it's okay. Every family assigns certain roles to its members. Sometimes those roles stick, even when you don't want them to. The great thing about being a child of God is that there's always the possibility for change. There's always a way to rise above the expectations that other people have set for us."

She nodded, still not convinced. "Thanks."

He tilted her chin up with his index finger. "You still don't believe me, do you?"

"I just want to be around people who will respect me for who I am. I don't want other people to think I'm expecting things from them." Her statement was aimed just as much at Nate as it was anyone else in her life. Sometimes she did get the impression that Nate saw her as an obligation. That was the last thing she wanted to be to anyone.

The rest of their meal they ate in silence. Finally, Nate turned to her. "We better get going if we want to be back in time for the candlelight vigil for Suzy."

They pedaled back at a leisurely pace, but thoughts still turned over in Kylie's mind. When Nate hadn't responded to her last statement, that led her to believe that he agreed with it, that she was an obligation.

The sting couldn't happen soon enough. The moment her stalker was behind bars, she'd leave Yorktown and Nate behind. She'd put a close to this entire chapter of her life and simply pretend it hadn't happened. Her cooking show would resume. Maybe she would become nationally syndicated. She'd prove to everyone that she could succeed on her own.

At the sound of a car accelerating behind her, she moved to the shoulder of the road. Cars had been passing them all day and had been more than willing to share the road with them and the other bikers who were out.

The engine revved behind them and Kylie glanced over her shoulder. Just as she looked back, the car charged forward.

"Watch out!" Nate gestured toward the grassy area beside them.

Kylie pumped her legs to get out of the way of the oncoming car. Her bike tires hit the grass and rolled toward the woods along the road.

The car sounded close, too close. She glanced over her shoulder. The vehicle headed toward them. Was the driver trying to run them over?

Nate maneuvered his bike so that he was between Kylie and the oncoming vehicle

Kylie feared it wouldn't make a difference. They'd never make it to the woods before the car slammed into them.

18

*J*ust as they reached the tree line, the car clipped Nate before turning sharply and speeding away.

Nate and Kylie crashed to the ground.

Was Nate hurt? Kylie untangled herself from the bike and knelt beside him. A gash split his temple and blood trickled down his face. Her eyes traveled to his leg, where the car had hit him. His pants were ripped at the calf and blood stained them.

"Nate! Are you okay?" She cradled his head in her lap, trying to elevate his wound.

He tried to raise himself, but pain etched his features. "That was no accident. Whoever was behind that wheel was trying to run us down."

"Why would they do that?"

He closed his eyes. "I have no idea."

Kylie pressed her lips together, worry over Nate superseding any other thoughts. "I need your phone, Nate. I'm going to call an ambulance—and the police."

"I don't need an ambulance."

"You have a terrible cut on your leg, Nate. And your head is bleeding."

"Are you okay?" He looked up at her and the concern Kylie saw in his eyes touched her.

"I'm fine. Thanks to you. You didn't have to put yourself between me and the car."

"Of course I did. I wouldn't be able to forgive myself if something happened to you."

"Or you're afraid my brother wouldn't forgive you."

He shook his head and placed his hand over hers, which rested on his cheek. "It has nothing to do with your brother and everything to do with you."

Kylie's face flushed and she looked away, unsure of how to take that comment. "I need your cell phone. I'm calling 911."

Kylie explained to the operator what had happened and she was told that help was on its way.

She clicked the phone shut and stroked Nate's hair, trying to comfort him.

The crash kept replaying in her mind.

"I'm fine, Kylie." He tried to sit up again, but his face squeezed in pain.

She pushed him back down. "Stay still until help gets here. Head injuries can be serious." She glanced at his leg again and saw more blood. Was it broken? How were his ribs? "We could have been killed," she mumbled.

"But we weren't."

"Why would someone do that?" An image of her stalker came to mind. No, she told herself. He'd never tried to hurt her. Not really. He just tried to scare her. Of course, maybe she'd upset him by coming here.

She looked down the road, waiting for an ambulance to appear. "Maybe the accident had to do with Suzy's disappearance. Or maybe the car's driver was drunk. Hard to say."

"With the accuracy he came at us with, I'd say he wasn't drinking."

Kylie glanced down at Nate's still perceptive eyes. "Did you get a good look at him?"

"The windows were tinted. I got the license plate number, though."

Of course he'd gotten the license plate number. He was Nate, always prepared, the perfect protector.

Nate tilted his head back until his gaze fully met hers. "This reminds me of the first time we met."

Kylie saw a twinkle in his eyes. Maybe he was okay.

"The first time we met?" That day already seemed like so long ago.

"You know, when you ran from me and Darlene clobbered me over the head with a rolling pin?"

Kylie tried not to smile. "Oh, yeah, I remember. I still feel bad about that."

Sirens in the distance caught Kylie's ear. A few seconds later, an ambulance and two sheriff cars appeared.

Relief filled her. Finally Nate would get the help he needed. She'd never forgive herself if something happened to him because of her.

"I don't need a wheelchair." Nate had already told the nurse that three times. She still insisted that a wheelchair was appropriate for his release.

Sure, he had sixteen stitches in his leg, four on his forehead and bruised ribs. He was going to be sore for a while. But he didn't need to be treated like an invalid.

"I'll help him out," Kylie said.

Nate glanced at her, wondering how well her one-hundred-pound frame would hold him up. It hardly seemed possible. But he didn't say anything. As long as he wasn't in a wheelchair.

Finally the stern-faced nurse gave a curt nod, along with a scowl, and signed the release paper. Kylie slipped an arm around his waist and began helping him toward the door. Her concern for him touched him.

Kylie had hardly left his side since the accident —the only time being when the doctor insisted on checking her out also. Thankfully, she only had a scraped elbow. It could have been so much worse. He cringed, not letting his mind go there.

His heart squeezed with sorrow anyway. He couldn't lose Kylie. He'd begun to care about her, but he didn't realize the extent of his feelings until the car had charged at them.

The sheriff was running a check on the license plate numbers now, but Nate guessed it wouldn't turn up anything.

"You doing okay?" Kylie's tiny arm was still

around his waist and his arm still draped over her shoulder.

He put just enough weight on her that she wouldn't suspect he was holding back. He kept his expression neutral so she wouldn't know how much pain jolted through him with every step.

"I'm fine. Nothing some pain medicine wouldn't cure."

"You're going to have to take it easy for a few days, you know."

"That's going to be near impossible, since we're short-staffed."

"I think Carrie's feeling better, and I'll get Harvey to come in again. We can handle it for a few days."

"I can't let you guys do that."

"You're going to let us do it. You need to rest, maybe just work in the office, if you have to work at all."

"You're getting bossy, aren't you?" The start of a smile twitched at his lip.

"I just know how stubborn you are."

He stopped outside of the hospital doors and turned toward Kylie. She lifted her eyes up to him, waiting for whatever he had to say. How did he tell her that he was falling for her?

He'd been a fool to ever think she was anything

like Deanna. Kylie was one of the best things God had ever brought into his life. But how did he tell her that?

"Kylie." He paused and ran his fingers down the outline of her cheek. Her cheeks flushed.

"Yes?" Her voice sounded whisper-soft.

"I . . . you—" Before he could finish, a car honked beside them.

Harvey and Darlene pulled up in front of the hospital, and upon stopping, Darlene hurried from the car toward them. She touched Nate's face like a mother would her child's.

"Oh, dear. I'm so glad you two are okay. I can't believe someone did that to you. What's going on in this town? First Suzy and now this. I just don't understand." She shook her head, and her lips pulled down in a frown.

Kylie grimaced, and Nate couldn't help but wonder what she was thinking. He hoped she didn't think the crimes had any connection to her. Both crimes had happened since she came here, and she was connected in both of the events. But that didn't mean any of this was her fault.

"The sheriff and his team will figure out what's going on. It just takes time sometimes." Nate opened the door to the backseat of the sedan and lowered himself inside. Pain screamed through each muscle. He definitely needed to take some more of the pain medication as soon as he could.

He didn't miss the glance that Kylie and Darlene exchanged. Maybe he wasn't doing as good of a job as he'd hoped of covering up his discomfort. A moment later, Kylie climbed in beside him.

Nate leaned his head against the back of the seat, trying his best to get comfortable. "I appreciate the ride back."

"It's the least we can do." Darlene glanced behind her at Nate, giving him that same motherly look that he loved her for. Sometimes having people in your life that worried about you felt nice.

Nate glanced at his watch. One hour until the candlelight prayer vigil began on the beachfront. He wanted to be there to support Simon and his family. And, if the sheriff called for search parties to go out tomorrow, as Nate suspected he might do, he wanted to be the first one in line, with or without his injuries.

"You're going to still try and make it to the vigil, aren't you?" Concern caused a little dimple to form on Kylie's chin.

"I need to be there," Nate said.

She reached for his hand and squeezed it. "I

want to be there too. I keep praying that Suzy will come traipsing into the restaurant sometime and admit that this was all a big misunderstanding."

"Suzy could very well do that. I pray nothing's happened to the girl, but she's always been a bit flighty," Harvey said. "I can say that because I've known her since she was in diapers when Darlene conned me into working in the toddler class at church."

"I might think the same thing, that Suzy was simply being irresponsible, if it weren't for her car being found in the parking lot," said Nate. "Too many things aren't adding up, and I think something's wrong—really wrong."

"I just want our little town to return to normal." Darlene waved her hand toward the window, where they passed a row of peaceful-looking houses. "None of this crime that we've had lately."

Nate's cell phone rang and he pulled it off his belt. He recognized the sheriff's number and answered.

The sheriff got right to the point. "The car that tried to run you off the road was stolen from Williamsburg."

"I figured that, since the license plates were visible," Nate said. "No luck locating it yet to see if whoever stole it left any evidence behind?"

"Not yet, but we will. I'm glad neither you nor that young lady was hurt. I feel like the whole town is being turned upside down lately. I don't like it."

Everyone in town seemed to feel the same way. They were ready for all of this nonsense to stop.

They hung up and Nate told Kylie the news. Apprehension tightened her features again. She closed her eyes and nodded solemnly.

He wanted to tell her that none of this was her fault, but he couldn't with Harvey and Darlene within listening distance. He had to remain the only person in Yorktown who knew the real reason for Kylie being here. Instead, he squeezed Kylie's hand, hoping she'd get his subtle message. She opened her eyes and offered a weak smile.

Finally, they arrived back at the restaurant. Nate thanked Harvey and Darlene before leading Kylie inside. He needed to check on the progress of the water main break. And he still hadn't checked all of his produce to make sure he had enough to last the week. He'd foolishly skipped working the past two days, and tomorrow, when the restaurant opened again, he'd regret it. Still, he didn't regret any of the time he'd spent with Kylie.

She planted herself in the hallway leading to his office and put her hands on her hips. "You need to lie down."

He would have put his hands on his hips also, but the action would hurt too badly. "I've got stuff to do that can't wait. Plus, the vigil is soon. I don't have time to rest before that."

"Just lie down then. I'm not saying you have to sleep. I'm just saying you need to take it easy."

Fire flashed in her eyes and Nate knew better than to argue. He hated to admit it, but he almost liked being bossed around . . . by Kylie, at least. It had been a long time since he'd had someone who wanted to take care of him for a change. He was so used to taking care of other people.

He nodded. "You win. I'll lie down."

Her eyes widened, as if she were surprised by his easy surrender. That look was quickly replaced by stubbornness, though. "And remember—you can *just* lie down. You can't sleep. Not with the head injury."

"It seems like we just had this conversation last week. Oh, wait, I think we did." He smiled, trying to lighten the mood.

Kylie scowled and pointed upstairs. "I'll come get you at five for the prayer vigil."

He saluted her before starting up the stairs. As he climbed up to his apartment, an image of what life would be like after Kylie returned to Kentucky flashed in his mind. Lonely. Empty. Sad.

He trudged up the remainder of the steps, each lift of his leg heavier than the last.

19

For the past hour, Kylie had hardly been able to stand looking at Nate. Every time she glanced up and saw that mesmerizing look in his eyes, she wanted nothing more than to reach up and kiss him. The thought was ridiculous. Nate Richardson was not the type of man she needed to be with.

Or was he?

She tried to occupy herself in her apartment for the forty-five minutes she had before the vigil. But, as she often did, she found herself pacing, trying to sort out the thoughts floating around in her mind. She kept thinking that maybe once her stalker was behind bars or she went back to Kentucky, then she'd find peace.

But maybe it was possible to find peace in the midst of the storm. Maybe peace wasn't something you found based on your external circumstances, but something that could be obtained from the inside.

That's what she'd found when she had cancer. She'd found that peace that passed all understanding. Why had she abandoned her faith as soon as she went into remission? Was it easier to rely on God in the hard times and easy to forget about Him in the good times? But she'd been going through the trial of her life lately and she just couldn't bring herself to cling to her Creator in the way she should.

Had her view of God somehow been skewed by her past relationships? Had she begun to think of God like she thought of Colin? It seemed possible. She always felt like God was trying to teach her lessons, like He'd given her free will but He tried to bend that free will whatever chance He got. She'd begun feeling suffocated by His presence instead of reveling in it.

Yes, she had let Colin mangle her view of God.

Why hadn't she seen that before?

"Lord, I'm so sorry," she whispered. "I've lost track of You, who You are and how much You love me. I began lumping You in with everyone else who came at me like I was fragile." God didn't think she was fragile, not with all the obstacles He handed her.

At once, her heart felt lighter.

God was with her every step of the way. No matter what happened on this journey, she could rest assured that He was in control and that He would take care of her. The peace she'd been so desperately missing covered her heart like a healing balm.

Why had she been too bullheaded to realize that? Why was she so stubborn that she wanted to do things her way, even when she knew her way wasn't the best way?

"Thank you, Lord." She wiped the tears from her eyes. "For loving me despite my shortcomings."

A glance at her watch showed her she had five minutes before the vigil. She touched up her makeup, which was nonexistent at this point, and ran a brush through her hair. A glance in the mirror revealed blood on her shirt. Her heart lurched. Nate's. She shuddered.

As she changed into something clean, she couldn't get the memory of the accident out of her head. The sound of a car barreling toward her. The rush of wind as their bikes tumbled. Seeing Nate lying on the grass. Wondering if he was alive.

A tear popped into the corner of her eye.

She cared for Nate more than she'd suspected.

"Lord, will You give me Your peace on my relationships as well?"

A rap at her door caused her to look at her watch again. Apparently, Nate had beaten her at being ready. When she saw him on the other side of the door, her heart raced. Without thinking, she stepped toward him and right into his arms.

"Are you okay?" he asked.

Kylie felt him tense, as if worried.

She nodded and didn't let go. "Yeah, I'm okay. I'm just glad you're not hurt any more than you are."

He tightened his embrace and kissed the top of her head. "I'm glad you're okay too, Kylie."

They stayed there a moment, simply holding one another. Kylie had to admit that it felt good to feel sheltered and protected. If there was one thing she could say about Nate, it was that he was like a soldier keeping guard over her. Never had she appreciated the act more.

When Nate released her from the hug, Kylie immediately missed the feel of his arms around her. His eyes met hers and she wondered what he was thinking. Still, words would have ruined the moment. Instead, he took her hand as they walked down the steps and outside. The air had a bit of chill to it since the sun had set, and Kylie felt thankful when Nate pulled her close. When they arrived on the beachfront, Kylie was surprised to see what a large crowd had gathered.

"It looks like everyone in Yorktown is here," Nate whispered.

They joined the throngs of people on the sandy shores. Someone handed them candles and someone else came with a lighter. A tiny flame danced on the white stick of wax.

Kylie looked around at those gathered. The crowd stretched as far as the pier. She spotted Harvey and Darlene, as well as some people who frequented the restaurant and others from church. A lot of young people—many of whom probably went to school with Suzy—wept together in groups.

A small sound system had been set up on a platform in front of them, and the pastor from Nate's church tapped on the microphone. Meanwhile, two different news vans had pulled up and cameramen, as well as reporters armed with microphones, mingled in the crowds, talking to anyone who knew Suzy.

Was the person guilty in her disappearance here in this crowd? Had they come to watch what transpired this evening, taking delight in the mourning around them?

The sheriff and a couple of his deputies were there, hopefully thinking those same questions.

The pastor tapped the microphone again and then cleared his throat. "We're gathered here tonight to pray for Suzy Hoffman. Many of you here tonight know Suzy from school or church or work. Others don't know Suzy at all, but you just came out of concern for a priceless member of our community. To all of you, the Hoffman family is thankful. It's times like this when communities are at their strongest, when they come together for a common cause . . ."

As he talked, people began passing out flyers with Suzy's picture on it. A tear came to Kylie's eyes when she saw her friend's picture. She lifted up another silent prayer for Suzy's safety. Nate's arm slipped around her waist and he pulled her closer.

After the pastor spoke, Yorktown's mayor took a turn, then one of Suzy's classmates and finally her father. Kylie's heart broke for the man, who could hardly keep his voice steady.

"I'm offering a reward of $10,000 to anyone who comes forward with information about Suzy's whereabouts. I beg you all, please, if you know anything—anything at all—about where my daughter is, please let the authorities know. Suzy is, and always has been, a precious gift to her mother and me, who were told we'd never have children . . ."

A teen got up and began singing some hymns and everyone joined in solemnly. Kylie closed her eyes and softly sang a hymn that, appropriately, was about peace.

Nate's gaze wandered the crowd again, as it had every few minutes this evening. He watched for anyone acting suspiciously or who seemed out of place. Most of the people around him he knew from growing up here in Yorktown.

His eyes zeroed in on a man standing back from the crowd. The man's hands were tucked into the pockets of his jeans and his eyes held a certain aloofness that made Nate suspicious. The first chance Nate had to talk to the sheriff, he'd bring the man to his attention.

Nate turned back toward the crowd, his head pounding. The pain medication he'd taken had begun to kick in, making him feel light-headed.

Perhaps he should have waited until after the candlelight vigil.

While people still sang, Simon pushed through the crowd, headed toward Nate. Suzy's disappearance had taken a toll on Simon. The lines around his eyes seemed deeper, his hair whiter. Nate greeted him with a hug.

Simon kept a hold of his hand as he began speaking, "Nate, the TV crew is looking for someone to talk to about Suzy. Would you mind? I know she thought the world of you."

He glanced at Kylie, who nodded. Nate would have to make sure Kylie stayed out of the limelight. The last thing she needed was her picture plastered all over the TV.

"Do you mind going to the pier? That way we'll get the crowd in the background." the reporter, who looked fresh out of college, asked.

Nate nodded. He glanced over at the man who'd been standing back from the crowd. He was gone.

Nate scanned the crowd, but the man was nowhere. His guard went up stronger than before.

He took Kylie's hand, the action feeling as natural as if they'd done it every day for the past year, as they walked across the sandy beach toward the pier. Once they walked down the wooden planks, Kylie stopped before reaching the end.

Plenty of townspeople still remained there, leaning against the rails and looking over the water. Nate would try to keep one eye on her as he did the interview. He'd also keep one eye out for the mysterious stranger.

Kylie glanced at the crowds on the shore and decided they would make a good background for Nate's interview, especially with all of the candles lit. The moon reflected off the water, and the bridge in the background always looked statuesque.

Kylie looked over at Nate, at the intense look in his eyes as he spoke with the reporter. She smiled. Despite everything that had happened, she was glad that she'd come here to Yorktown. What would it be like to leave? Heaviness pressed on her heart. Her life was back in Kentucky, but apparently her heart had found a home here . . .

People behind her jostled against each other and against her, as more people joined them on the pier. Kylie moved closer to the railing and leaned her elbows there, looking over at the dark water below.

Nate had just been talking about how cool the water still was, how it didn't warm up until June. He talked about how this river was one of the deepest channels in the United States. She closed her eyes and pictured being out on this water with Nate, in his boat on a lazy Sunday afternoon.

A hand pressed on her shoulder, snapping her from her thoughts.

Before she could turn and see who was behind her, the hand shoved her. Her body lifted. She tried to grab the railing. But she couldn't.

Suddenly, she was falling.

Kylie screamed and tried to prepare herself for the icy splash into the dark water below.

20

*N*ate heard a scream, then a splash. He whipped around. His gaze flew to the water. Had someone fallen? Jumped in as a prank? He gripped the railing, waiting for a face to emerge from the dark depths below.

His eyes darted toward Kylie.

Her spot by the pier was empty.

He looked back at the water, his heart pounding in his ears.

A dark-haired figured emerged, but only for a moment. The black water consumed the person like a hungry monster.

Kylie.

He waited for her to emerge again. She didn't.

Nate grabbed the reporter. "Call 911."

He stripped off his jacket, stepped over the pier, and dove into the river. The cold water sent a shock through his body. His already aching and sluggish limbs jolted with adrenaline.

He emerged to the surface, treading water, gulping in breaths.

He took note of the pier behind him, tried to keep a point of reference.

Where was Kylie? The top of the river looked smooth, with no signs of anyone else in the water. He waited for bubbles to emerge, to let him know where Kylie was.

Lord, help me find her.

A stream of bubbles finally surfaced. He plunged underwater, his arms reaching out for something—anything—that could be Kylie.

Nothing.

His lungs burned. He surfaced. Found his point of reference. Took a breath. Dove back under. Swam toward the pier.

Still nothing.

She couldn't stay under water this long without air. She wouldn't survive. He had to find her.

He dove once more and reached the bottom of the river. The sharp edge of a rock scraped his hand. Then seaweed . . . Or was that hair? He reached again, his lungs aching. Hair. That was hair!

Lungs still burning, he reached forward. A hand? Yes.

He wrapped his arm around Kylie's waist and propelled himself upward. At the surface, he gasped for air. Looked over. Saw Kylie's lifeless face.

He had to do CPR. Fast.

The shore looked miles away. It didn't matter. He had to get her there as soon as possible. He pulled Kylie onto his chest and began swimming on his back with the current toward the shore.

Hasten my pace, Lord.

The pain medicine made him sluggish. He should never have taken it.

Lord, You can help me through this. Save her.

A figure splashed in the water beside them, taking even strokes his way. His face appeared through the dark.

John.

His friend reached out for Kylie.

"Nate, I've got her. An ambulance is here. Get yourself back to shore."

Thank You, Lord.

He reached the shore and pulled himself out of the icy water. Two paramedics surrounded him with a blanket, but he pushed past the men and rushed toward Kylie. She lay on the ground, even in the dark looking blue and lifeless. Two paramedics pumped her heart with their hands, blew breath into her lungs. Nate knelt beside her.

Lord, help her. Breathe breath into her lungs. Fill her limbs with life.

His heart twisted at her still form. As a former Coast Guardsman, he'd seen too many circumstances like these. Some ended well and others didn't

Help this one end well, Lord.

As he said a silent amen, Kylie sputtered. He sucked in a breath, watching for the next sign of life. Finally, her eyes opened.

Praise God. Thank you.

"We've got to get you to the hospital." One of the medics placed a forceful hand on Nate's shoulder.

Nate reached forward, squeezed Kylie's hand. "Kylie . . ."

Her gaze connected with him. "Someone . . . pushed . . . me.

"We'll talk to the sheriff. He'll get to the bottom of this. We've just got to work on getting you well right now."

She nodded, but her gaze skittered toward the

pier, as if searching for a familiar face. Then she closed her eyes again. The paramedics hoisted her onto a gurney and carried her to a waiting ambulance. Nate stayed by her side.

"You need to put that blanket around you so you don't get hypothermia, sir." The medic handed him another blanket Nate threw it across his shoulders to humor the man. He'd worry about himself later. Right now, his only concern was Kylie. He should never have taken his eyes off of her. He should have known better.

Nate reached the ambulance and didn't bother to ask if he was welcome inside. He climbed in with Kylie.

John appeared at the doors, a familiar blanket around his shoulders and hair glistening from his dive into the river.

"John, tell the sheriff that Kylie was pushed," Nate said. "They need to question everyone at that pier. Don't let anyone go home before they're checked out."

John nodded as another ambulance broke through the crowd of onlookers. "Will do."

The doors closed, shutting out the outside world as they took off to the hospital—again. Nate squeezed Kylie's hand, ignoring the numbness that had settled through his bones. Feebly, Kylie opened her eyes and offered a weak smile before they put an oxygen mask over her face.

He smiled back, trying to reassure her that everything would be okay. He'd never admit that he feared now more than ever for her safety.

Kylie was thankful for the plastic inflatable blankets around her. What had the nurse called it? A bear hugger? A machine pumped warm air into its depths and warmed her core temperature. Warm soup had helped also. As Sunday turned into Monday her shivering had started to fade, but her head still ached uncontrollably.

As she listened to the electronic beep of her heartbeat in the hospital room, she couldn't help but thank God that this hadn't turned out differently. If Nate hadn't seen her go in . . . If John hadn't been nearby to help . . . If the ambulance hadn't arrived so quickly . . .

She stopped thinking about the what ifs, though. The important thing was that besides a concussion and hypothermia, she was going to be okay. A CT scan had shown no other injuries.

A knock sounded at the door and Detective Blackston stuck his head inside. "Is this a good time for some questions?"

Her mind was finally beginning to settle, to gain a bit of steadiness. She nodded and the detective stepped toward her, pad of paper in hand. He shifted at her bedside, a fatherly gaze washing over her.

"How are you feeling?"

She shrugged. "For the second time in twenty-four hours, I'm thankful to be alive, if that tells you anything." Her focus sharpened. "How's Nate? Have you talked to him? Is he okay?"

The detective nodded. "He's doing fine. I'm sure he'll be down here to see you as soon as he gets past the nurse who's keeping guard over him."

Kylie smiled, remembering the nurse from earlier with whom Nate had butted heads.

Kylie's smile dimmed. She was the reason Nate had been in these precarious positions.

"I'm glad you're okay, Kylie. I have to say that, at first, I thought these episodes were random. It's becoming clear that you're a target. Whoever is doing this even may even be targeting Suzy as a way of getting to you."

She shivered again, but not from hypothermia this time. Her gaze drifted to the clear nighttime sky outside her hospital window. "I've considered that also."

"I say that in no way to imply that you're to blame, Kylie."

She nodded, but she couldn't help but blame herself. If it hadn't been for her, Nate wouldn't be in this position. She continued to stare out the window, trying not to let the tears that had formed in her eyes roll down her cheeks.

The detective cleared his throat, as if uncomfortable. "I talked to your brother. He doesn't seem convinced that your stalker has found you here. I'm frankly at a loss for any other explanation, however."

Kylie wiped at her cheeks and looked at the detective again, knowing she couldn't feel sorry for herself. "I was cautious on the pier. I kept my eyes open all night, looking for anyone even remotely familiar. I didn't see anyone, detective. I turned my back for one minute to look out over the water when I felt someone shove me. Then I hit the water and I don't remember anything until I woke up on shore."

Detective Blackston nodded, his jaw set in a tight line. "No one's blaming you."

She squeezed the blankets around her more tightly. "Did anyone else on the pier see anything?"

"Unfortunately, the pier was crowded . . ."

"So, in other words, no. Whoever did this will get away with it."

"We're working our best men on this case. We're also going to check the video footage the news crews were shooting. We could find something there. Whoever's doing this will eventually screw up."

"Which means you anticipate that there will be more attempts on my life." Saying the words out loud caused a strange fear to grip her heart.

The detective drew in another deep breath before nodding solemnly. "That would seem likely, Kylie."

"Should I go back to Kentucky? Am I safer there?" Her mind raced through the possibilities.

"There's no way of knowing until we figure out if your stalker has followed you here. The sting is scheduled for Tuesday." He checked his watch. "Make that tomorrow. I want to wait and see what happens. In the meantime, I'll have a man stationed outside your door here at the hospital at all times."

"And I'll be here also," a deep, familiar voice said in the distance.

Kylie looked to the doorway and saw Nate. Her heart fluttered in ways she didn't expect. "You got past your bodyguard, I see."

He smiled. "Good to see you still have your sense

of humor." He came to the other side of her bed and took her hand. The warmth of his touch against her skin also warmed her heart.

"I'm glad you're okay, Nate. Thank you for . . . saving my life." Her voice caught as she said the words, and her words trailed off into a whisper.

Nate's eyes became swirling pools of emotions, fixed on Kylie. "You gave me a good scare, Kylie."

"We've got to stop scaring each other, then." She tried to manage a smile but wasn't sure if she succeeded.

Detective Blackston cleared his throat beside her and shifted his weight. "I think I have everything I need from both of you. If you think of anything else—"

"We'll give you a call." Nate looked away from her and finished filling in the blank for the detective.

When the detective left, Nate sat down on the bed beside her. His fingers stroked her hand, the action amazingly soothing. "You sure you're doing okay?"

Kylie nodded. "Yeah, I'm just trying to come to terms with the fact that someone is targeting me here in Yorktown. Do you think it's the same person who did this to me in Kentucky? It's the only thing that makes sense to me, but at the same time, the man in Kentucky never tried to harm me, only scare me."

Nate grimaced, his eyes getting that hard look they often took on. "The most logical explanation is that it's the same person."

She nodded, feeling that same heaviness settle over her heart.

"We're going to get through this, Kylie."

She squeezed his hand. "Thanks, Nate."

She didn't miss the "we" reference in his statement. It comforted her beyond reason to feel like she wasn't in this alone. She wanted to reach up, touch the edges of his face, feel the stubble of his five o'clock shadow on her fingertips.

Instead, she cleared her throat. "How's your friend John?"

"He's doing fine. They released him already."

"Thank goodness he was there."

They stared at each other for another minute, those unspoken words between them remaining unspoken. Why did she always seem to lose her words when it came to talking about whatever was developing between them? Nate couldn't seem to find the words either . . . or was she the only one feeling this way? Could she be imagining that he felt the same?

The phone on the nightstand rang and Nate plucked it from its holder. It was her brother. Nate handed the phone to her, and Kylie had the strange suspicion that the two of them had already spoken.

"How you doing, sis?" As usual, worry etched the deep strains of his voice.

"I've been better."

He paused, and Kylie could picture him, his jaw hard and his gaze steely as he thought about what had happened to her. A moment later, he said, "The sting is Tuesday. We'll catch this guy, Kylie. We will. If it's the last thing I do, I'll put this man behind bars."

"Not if he's in Yorktown."

"It's highly unlikely. It doesn't seem possible that he could discover you're there. How many people know the real reason you're there, besides Nate and the detective? Anyone?"

"No, no one. Except . . ." Her mind formed an image of that day in the restaurant, of the staring customer who turned out to be . . .

"Except who?"

She blew out a breath. "The producer from Cuisine TV. I had to admit to him that I was here under unusual circumstances and plead for privacy. But there's no way he would . . ."

"It could be anyone, Kylie."

She twisted the phone cord around her finger. "What about Colin? Has anyone seen him lately?"

"Do you think he could be the one? I mean, I never liked the guy, but . . ."

Kylie shook her head and then stopped. "I don't know anything anymore, to be honest. You'd think if Colin were here, I'd recognize him. I'd see him and know."

"I'll have someone drive past his place, see if he's there. Maybe I'll even do it myself."

"It couldn't hurt, I guess."

"I'll call you tomorrow, Kylie. The cooking demonstration is at noon, so we'll be calling after that with an update."

After she hung up, she found Nate staring at her. "Who's Colin?"

"An ex-boyfriend."

"You think he could be your stalker?"

She shrugged. "The thought has crossed my mind. That's what makes me feel so crazy. I've never seen this person's face. He could be anyone."

"Did you have a hard breakup? Was he upset?"

That day flashed in her mind. "You could say that. He was used to me doing whatever he told me to do, for the most part. I was foolish and tried not to rock the boat, so I usually did listen to him. He couldn't believe that I would break up with him. He kept saying I would change my mind."

Nate scowled again. "What happened after that? Did he leave you alone? Or did he pester you to take him back?"

Kylie searched her memories and then shrugged. "He basically left me alone. I do think that he thought I'd eventually come back to him. But I didn't. I had no desire to."

"And he never spoke to you about it again?"

She almost said no, when she remembered one instance. "There was an evening when he showed up at my office at the studio, looking upset and disheveled. He threatened to sabotage my show and convince the network to shut it down."

"What did you say?"

"I told him I'd contact my lawyer."

Nate smiled. "I bet he didn't like that."

"No, he didn't. I've never seen him so angry, actually. We didn't speak again."

And with that thought, she fell into a restless sleep, tainted with nightmares of a faceless man chasing her. At various times, the faceless man's features morphed into Colin's, or even Frank's. When would this real-life nightmare be over?

21

When Kylie woke sometime during the night, she spotted Nate stretched out in the recliner in her hospital room. His breathing was even and a flimsy blanket, one far too small for his build, lay across his arms and chest.

She smiled, grateful that he cared enough to not leave her side. He must be in agony himself, having endured the hit-and-run, as well as diving into the frigid water to rescue her. Yet he seemed concerned only about her well-being.

Had she really misread the man that badly when they'd first met? She'd assumed he was just like her ex-boyfriend, that he'd try to control her and take away her independence. Nate was anything but that.

Thank you for sending him to me, Lord.

"Hi," Nate said. A smile spread across his face.

Kylie looked away as her face heated. She hadn't realized he'd awoken, and she'd been staring, yet in her own little world at the same time. "Thanks for camping out here."

He pulled himself up in the recliner and ran a hand over his face. "I don't think you should be alone. Not until this guy is behind bars."

Something deep, dark flickered in his eyes. The look that had crossed his face many times before, usually when someone mentioned the danger Kylie faced, appeared again.

She grabbed his hand and squeezed, imploring him with her eyes to share his thoughts. "What's going on, Nate? Will you let me know what you're thinking?"

He looked down at their hands. "I thought I was going to lose you."

"But you didn't."

He shook his head. "Kylie . . . I don't know what your brother told you, but . . . my last rescue mission was a tough one, to say the least."

"He didn't tell me anything, Nate."

"There was a yacht that capsized. A whole family on board. It was at night and there was this awful storm and we were miles from land, our helicopter barely able to stay in the air because the winds were so strong."

"Sounds scary."

"I saved the two young kids first. Then I saved the husband—he was injured pretty severely and couldn't swim on his own. I promised the mom I would come back for her." His face twisted in agony. "Before I could, the boat went under. I searched the waters for as long as I could looking for her. But we had to get back to land."

Kylie squeezed his hand, her heart flinching. "You did everything you could, Nate."

His hollow eyes met hers. "I broke a promise, though. I told the woman I'd be back for her. Today, her kids don't have a mom. I grew up without a mom and I know how bad it hurts. It's all my fault."

"It's hardly your fault. Maybe the family shouldn't have been out at that hour. Maybe you could blame it on the storm that capsized the boat. But don't blame yourself. You tried to help."

He drew in a long, labored breath. "Afterward, I started drinking. I don't know why that mission affected me so much. Your brother was the only one who confronted me, let me see that I had to stop drinking away my problems. I got my life back on track, got right with God. But the guilt still doesn't go away."

Kylie pressed her fingers into his. "Nate, listen to me. If something happens to me, it won't be by any fault of yours. It's not your fault that some madman has been stalking me. It's not your fault that Suzy's missing. You have to stop blaming yourself."

His eyes—red, strained—pulled up to meet hers. "I felt like I was reliving that night again, Kylie. The water was dark. I couldn't find you."

"But you did." His concern touched deep places in her heart.

"I can't stand the thought that someone's doing this to you."

Kylie licked her lips, the realizations that God had laid on her heart pounding to the surface. "Nate, I really feel like God's been speaking to me lately. I'm a hardhead sometimes, but I've finally figured out that you can let circumstances determine who you are, or you can determine who you are through the circumstances. I'd somehow lost sight of that. Maybe you need to remember that, too. You saved three lives that night. You've saved countless others. Don't beat yourself up for the rest. You can't save everyone."

He hung his head a moment and nodded. Kylie

could see the struggle in him. She rested her hand on his head, running her fingers through his hair. He needed time to process everything. She knew that. And she needed time to recover from the day's traumas.

Kylie cleared her throat "Now that the water-main break is fixed, you probably need to go and get things ready to open the restaurant. I'm sure Darlene can pick me up or the deputy outside the door can give me a ride back."

He raised his head, his gaze still appearing burdened. "I can't open the restaurant tomorrow, Kylie. I can't open it with just Carrie, Harvey and me. It would be a disaster. Besides, I want to stay with you. I need to stay with you."

"But I know you depend on it for your income. I don't want to—"

"It's not a problem, Kylie. I have someone interested in buying the place. I'm supposed to meet with him this week. Maybe the place won't be my problem anymore."

Kylie remained silent a moment. "And what will you do?"

"Teach at the Coast Guard Training Center, I hope."

Guilt still gnawed at her. "That's great for the

future, but I'm sorry to put you in this position right now, Nate."

"I'm making my own choices, Kylie. Don't be sorry." His gaze held hers.

She swallowed, her throat suddenly feeling dry, and looked away, afraid that Nate was seeing too much of her soul. "Who's the buyer?"

Nate shrugged. "Someone who's always wanted to own his own restaurant. I don't know much about him except that he has the capital to buy the place. I guess he invested in some real estate before the market crashed and got out just in time. He thinks The Revolutionary Grill could be a real winner with some changes."

"Some changes?"

He shrugged again. "I guess it's none of my business what he does with the place after he buys it. He wants to modernize the grill. Add a bar. Maybe have an Italian theme."

"Italian? In Yorktown? That would just ruin the whole atmosphere of the restaurant." She paused and bit her lip, afraid she'd said too much or that her words would influence him. "But I guess that's none of my business either."

"You have a lot more passion for the place than I do. You have a right to an opinion."

Before she could respond, the nurse bustled into the room, took Kylie's vitals, and gave her another shot of pain medication into her IV. Before the nurse left the room, Kylie was out again.

Nate watched Kylie sleeping, grateful that she was alive and more determined than ever to figure out who the person was behind these attacks. Kylie's brother was worried. They'd talked after Kylie was admitted into the hospital and Bruce had confessed that much to Nate.

Nate prayed that the sting tomorrow was successful. But even then, if her stalker in Kentucky was caught, it wouldn't explain who was behind these attacks in Virginia.

His body ached in ways he didn't want to admit. Despite that, he stood, walked toward the door, and peered into the hallway. A sheriff's deputy still stood guard outside.

Feeling better, Nate closed the door and went back to the most uncomfortable recliner he'd ever sat in. Even though the nurse had brought him another blanket, it would do little to offer him comfort this evening. He pulled it around his shoulders and closed his eyes.

He woke up at 7:30 to the phone beside Kylie's bed ringing. He glanced at the time and saw that four hours had passed. Groggily, he pulled himself up and snatched the phone from its cradle. The voice on the other end informed him that it was Sebastian, a former chef at his restaurant. What could he be calling about? He glanced at Kylie and saw her starting to stir.

"Don't come to the restaurant today," Sebastian said.

Nate braced himself for whatever reason Sebastian would give him. Had something happened there also? Why didn't the sheriff tell him? "Why not?"

"I'm cooking there today."

"But you have another job."

"I'm taking a few days off to help out. It's no problem, Nate. Besides, I still remember when you helped me fix up my bike and didn't even charge me for the parts you bought. It's the least I can do."

"The offer is kind, Sebastian, but I don't even have enough staff to fill the other positions right now. There's no way we can open."

"Carrie called in some people she knows. We can do it. We want to. We know the restaurant means a lot to you, but you need to take care of yourself right now."

"That's kind of you. I don't know what to say."

"Don't say anything. Just let us do this."

When he hung up, Kylie gave him a quizzical glance. "What was that about?"

Nate filled her in.

Kylie grinned. "It sounds like you've impacted a lot of people."

"It sure doesn't feel like it."

"Look at the fruit you're sowing."

He looked into the distance. "Maybe I should tell them not to bother . . ."

"Of course you shouldn't. Let them help you. Remember, that's what life is about. I think you told me that not too long ago." She smiled, her face still a little drowsy from sleep, but never having looked so beautiful.

Just as the sun was beginning to set, the doctor released Kylie. Nate insisted on wheeling her out to John's awaiting car, even though she put up a fuss.

Kylie smiled at John as they approached, appreciation showing in each motion. "John, how are you? Are you okay? Thank you so much for everything."

John smiled in return. "It's no problem, Kylie. I've done it for strangers before. Doing it for you guys was a no-brainer."

Inside the car, Nate tucked Kylie into the nook of his arm. She leaned against him, obviously not feeling one hundred percent yet.

"Any updates on who did this?" John put the car into Drive and took off.

Nate shook his head. "Not yet. The sheriff assures us he's working on it. I just know we've got to catch whoever is doing this—and soon."

"I think everyone in town agrees with you."

Comfortable silence filled the car. Kylie's head still rested against Nate and her eyes closed. Nate prayed that her recovery would be swift and pain-less. The body could only take so much trauma.

John bypassed downtown Yorktown and instead crossed the Coleman Bridge.

Kylie peeked an eye open. "Where are we going?"

"John offered to let us stay at his place until all of this clears up. I think it's a good idea." He hoped Kylie agreed and wouldn't put up too much of an argument. He didn't have the strength to fuss with her today.

Thankfully, she nodded. Nate guessed she was probably too exhausted to argue, also. A day like Sunday would do that to anyone. It had robbed them physically, emotionally . . . but perhaps renewed them spiritually? It was funny how hard times could do that.

After crossing the bridge, they turned down a wooded street leading to some cottages nestled on the banks of the York River, opposite Yorktown. John pulled into his gravel driveway, the tires rumbling with each inch, and came to a gentle stop. His house stood two stories, with a pier stretching into the water and a small boat bobbing at the end.

Nate helped Kylie from the car, careful with each movement not to exacerbate her injuries. She had little to say, which just proved that the medication was still affecting her.

"I'll show you to your rooms. They're nothing fancy," John said.

"They'll be perfect. We appreciate you letting us stay here."

Nate kept a hand on Kylie's elbow to steady her as she walked upstairs.

Kylie was already looking tired, even from the short ride from the hospital, so they left her to lie down. The two men went downstairs to talk. Nate had already filled John in on the situation. Nate knew if he could trust anyone in this situation, it was John. They'd had each other's backs more than once.

"You've fallen for her, haven't you?" John asked, seated across from him with a mug of coffee in hand.

Nate gripped his coffee with both hands and raised his eyes. "Is it that obvious?"

"It's obvious that you care about her."

After a moment of thought, Nate nodded. "I do."

"Have you told her yet?"

"I'm just waiting for the right time. She's not going to be in Yorktown long. I want her to make her own decisions about staying or going."

John leaned back and draped an arm over the back of the chair. "So, do the police have any leads about who is targeting you and Kylie?"

"There's a sting tomorrow in Kentucky. We're hoping that's the end of this. There's no way this man should know that Kylie is here in Virginia. I have no idea how the crimes taking place here are connected to her—or to us, I should say. I'm connected just as much as she is."

"If it's not her stalker, then who is it?"

Nate shrugged, that same weight returning to his chest. "I don't know. I wish I did. I wish I did."

Kylie slept until the next morning, slumber easily finding her. Knowing that Nate and John weren't far away helped, as did the pain medicine she'd taken.

As she crawled out of bed, muscles she didn't realize she had ached and pulled and whimpered. It took longer than she would have liked to stretch and find her footing. She crept into the hallway and spotted a bathroom two doors down.

She barely recognized the person staring back at her in the mirror. One eye was bruised and a huge knot, along with a gash, streaked across her forehead. Her forearm was bandaged from a cut she'd gotten, presumably when being dragged out of the water. Her hair, usually long and wavy, was now frizzy and matted. And she had no clothes to change into or even a brush for her hair. Not exactly the way to impress someone, but she had no other choice.

She splashed some water on her face and found a rubber band to pull her hair back with. She padded downstairs, where John and Nate were drinking coffee at a breakfast table in the kitchen. Beyond them, she caught a glimpse of the York River, sparkling and blue and beautiful.

"Good morning." Nate stood. "Can I get you some coffee?"

"That sounds great." She plopped at the table, more muscles and joints and bones aching. Even her eyes ached. "How are you guys?"

"Better than you, I'd say." John raised his coffee mug toward her.

Nate placed coffee in front of her and she greedily took a sip, hoping the caffeine would help the pounding in her head. The drink's warmth washed over her, and she welcomed the feeling like an old friend.

She closed her eyes and circled her hands around the cup. Today was the operation her brother had set up to catch her stalker. Her eyes searched the room for a clock. Eight-twenty. The sting would take place in less than four hours.

She closed her eyes and lifted a prayer that everything would go smoothly, that the man behind the threats on her life would be captured, arrested, thrown in jail. Before she said amen, a hand covered hers.

She looked up and saw Nate's warm, reassuring eyes on her.

"It will all be over soon," he assured her.

If only Kylie felt so sure. "We hope."

Her gaze connected with Nate's. Thank God He had sent Nate to her. She would have been lost without him over the past several days.

John cleared his throat and slid his chair back. He pointed toward the back door. "I have a few things to do outside. I'm keeping the doors locked and taking my keys with me. No one knows you're here, but just to be safe I want to keep everything around here secure."

Kylie got the message—both of the men still feared for her safety. She nodded and took another sip of her coffee as John slipped outside.

Kylie's gaze went back to Nate. She took in the bruises and the stitches—all the injuries he'd gotten because of her. The fact that he'd put his life in danger for her only solidified her feelings for the man. If only she felt confident that he felt the same way.

"Thanks for being there for me over the past couple of days, Nate. I really appreciate everything you've done. I don't feel like I can tell you that enough."

"I'm just glad you're okay." He leaned forward and kissed her forehead. "You gave me a good scare."

Her cheeks warmed again. *You're acting like a schoolgirl around your crush, Kylie.* She cleared her throat, pushing her feelings down. "Any updates on who pushed me?"

Nate shook his head. "I called the detective before you woke up. All he could say was that they were checking out a few leads."

Kylie sighed and rolled her eyes. "That phrase is becoming old."

"The sheriff's department is competent. I know it may not feel like it sometimes, but they are. And they're doing everything they can to figure out what's going on."

"What about Suzy? Has anyone come forward with any leads?" Kylie gripped the mug tighter.

"Not yet. But there's still hope. There's always hope."

Kylie smiled. "Listen to you. Suddenly the optimist. I like it."

Nate reached for her hand and stroked her fingers. "That's thanks in part to you. You've shown me some of that hope."

The same heat rose again to her cheeks. "I don't know how much I had to do with that."

Nate's gaze remained on hers. "Everything. You had everything to do with it."

Kylie was doing her best to relax—doctor's orders—and to keep her mind off the sting that was supposed to have taken place thirty minutes ago. She flipped stations on the TV and lay back on the couch while Nate prepared lunch. Based on the smells drifting from the kitchen, Kylie guessed he was making steak, baked potatoes and garlic bread.

When the phone rang, Kylie sat up straight, her muscles tense. She listened as Nate answered but couldn't make out any more of the conversation. Was it her brother? If so, what was he telling Nate?

She stood and, as she walked toward the kitchen, Nate appeared with a huge smile.

He dangled the phone toward her. "They caught him."

Kylie half squealed, half moaned in delight and disbelief. Could it really be true? Could her nightmare be over?

Nate opened his arms and Kylie flew into them. He swirled her in a small circle and planted a light kiss on her temple. When he placed her back on the ground, she held on to him to steady herself and looked at the phone. She needed to hear the news directly from her brother. She took the handset from Nate and placed it to her ear.

"Bruce. Nate told me the news." She rubbed her

free hand on her jeans, realizing that she'd started to sweat. "Who was he?"

"He was a fan. FAN756 to be exact, just as we suspected. But we finally caught him."

She closed her eyes, but relief wouldn't quite come. "Are you sure you got the right guy?"

"Kylie, this guy had a little shrine set up at his house dedicated to you. His phone records show he's called you numerous times."

The man did sound like a slam-dunk match to her stalker. It would take a while for her to believe that her nightmare was over, though. "How'd you catch him? How did you know it was him?"

People mumbled in the background, and Kylie suspected her brother was still at the kitchen store where the demonstration took place. She imagined cops milling around and a crowd of onlookers wondering what was going on.

"He was in the crowd, standing at the back. He was sweating, as if he was nervous. He tried to sneak away early, but we caught him, said we wanted to ask him a few questions. He confessed to everything."

Kylie raised her eyebrows. "To everything? Really?"

"He said he's been following you for months, doing whatever he could to get close to you."

Kylie nodded. He'd confessed. That settled it . . . right? "Was he wearing the black hooded sweatshirt?"

"Black? No, I think it was more of a camouflage T-shirt. Why?"

Kylie's muscles tensed and her mind raced with a million thoughts, questions, denials. "Because my stalker always wore a black hooded sweatshirt."

Nate squeezed her arm, still at her side.

"Kylie, there's nothing to worry about. We got him." Bruce's voice left no room for question or doubt. That was her brother. Always sure of himself. "We'll still have to go to court, but he's owned up to everything, Kylie. You can finally relax. You can finally come home."

Why did hearing that she could come home make her heart throb with sadness? She hung up and saw Nate watching her curiously.

"You don't look happy," he said.

Kylie crossed her arms over her chest. "Something just doesn't feel right. The man who was stalking me always wore a black hooded sweatshirt. Why would he show up at the demonstration showing his face?"

"Maybe he knew he was a sure target if he wore the sweatshirt."

She nodded halfheartedly. "Maybe."

The phone jingled again. Was her brother calling back again so quickly? Had he forgotten to tell her something?

Nate answered, and Kylie saw his face darken. As soon as he hung up, she asked, "What's wrong?"

"Someone just threw a brick through the front window at the Grill."

22

*K*ylie, freshly showered and in clean clothes now, walked into the dining area at The Revolutionary Grill and spotted Nate sitting at a table with his back to her. Beyond him, the front window of the restaurant was covered with two pieces of plywood. The glass on the floor, as well as the broken ceramic from a vase and some splintered wood, had been cleaned up. The police had left and all was quiet.

Questions still nagged at Kylie, though. Was this vandalism connected with her stalker? The right man was behind bars, wasn't he? FAN756 had confessed. Kylie shook her head, unsure what to think. The only other conclusion she could muster was that he tied in with Suzy's disappearance somehow.

As she approached Nate, Kylie sensed his frustration. She placed her hands lightly on his shoulders. She rubbed the tense muscles at his neck for a moment before sliding her hand down his arm as she made her way to the seat across from him. As she sat down, she grasped his hand. She'd bring up Suzy later. For now, she wanted to talk about his restaurant.

"You can get past this, Nate," she told him softly.

"Maybe I don't want to get past it, Kylie." He looked up and met her gaze. "Maybe this should just be the end of the road for me. I should just put this restaurant out of its misery."

"Even if the sale doesn't go through and you close the restaurant, I think you should end it on a positive note. Fix the place up and let it go out as a success."

He pulled back his lip in doubt. "You're always an optimist, aren't you?" He leaned forward and kissed her gently.

"I thought some of that was rubbing off on you." Her lips curled in a half smile. "Nate, I just think if you close the place down like this, you're always going to remember your time here as being a failure, which is the furthest thing from the truth. If you close, close strong."

He tugged at her hand until she stood and met him in an embrace.

"You're one of the best things that ever happened to this place," he mumbled into her hair. "Do you know that? It won't be the same without you. I won't be the same."

Kylie's heart lurched. She wasn't sure she'd be the same when she went back to Kentucky either. Her heart seemed to be making itself home here in Yorktown, with Nate.

The front door opened, indicated by the tingling of the bell. Nate pulled back slightly and turned his head toward the sound.

"I'm sorry, we're closed—" He stopped midsentence.

Kylie's gaze cut to the woman in the doorway, who stood with wide eyes and pouty lips. With her bobbed light-brown hair, cut to her jawline, and tall lanky figure, she wasn't necessarily beautiful but instead striking.

"Deanna." Nate dropped his arms from around Kylie. He stepped toward the woman. "What are you doing here?"

"I'm interrupting something." Her soft, delicate

voice indicated she could break at any moment. Kylie thought for sure she saw tears in the woman's eyes when she pointed behind her to the front door. "I should leave."

Nate shook his head, appearing to have all but forgotten about Kylie. "No, stay. What are you doing here, Deanna?"

Deanna? Kylie didn't have to ask. She could tell by Nate's expression that this was the woman who'd broken his heart.

Deanna glanced at Kylie before her gaze fluttered back to Nate.

"I was hoping we could talk." This time the woman's gaze firmly met Kylie's. "In private."

Kylie refrained from frowning and instead nodded, taking a step back. "I'll be upstairs packing my things."

Before Nate could refuse—not that he was going to—Kylie hurried away. Maybe everything was working out for the best. She was going back to Kentucky and Nate's old girlfriend had showed up. Life would resume as normal for both of them.

But could Kylie's life ever really feel normal without Nate by her side?

"I didn't expect to see you again." Nate stared at Deanna. What had brought her back here to Yorktown? Caution caused his spine to straighten, put him on his guard. Deanna wasn't here to simply say hello. He knew her better than that.

"I had to see you again." Her hand flipped through her hair, moving the strands away from her eyes. Her pleading gaze connected with his in a look he'd fallen for too many times before. She nodded toward the window. "What happened?"

"Vandals."

Her gaze softened. "I'm sorry. I know that's a setback for you."

Nate had fallen too many times for those looks. Though she'd said generally the same thing as Kylie, somehow the words sounded more genuine coming from Kylie.

"We'll get past it. It's life." He glanced behind him, hoping Kylie was still nearby. She'd already disappeared up the stairs, though. He should have pleaded with her to stay, insisted even. But the conversation he needed to have with Deanna, he needed to do alone, as much as it pained him to let Kylie go. "So, tell me exactly why you had to see me again. You certainly didn't seem too concerned when you up and left without an explanation."

She looked to the ground, as if guilty, but Nate could see through her masquerade. "That was a mistake. I knew it the moment I got into my car."

"Then why didn't you turn back around?"

She bit her lower lip. "It's not that easy." She stepped toward him and put her hand on his chest. "Nate, you've always been the one. I just didn't see it. I was a fool."

"No, I was the fool." He shook his head.

Deanna's eyes brightened and she raised her gaze to meet his.

Nate met her gaze firmly. "I let you use me for far too long, and then you left when a better opportunity came along."

Her face pulled downward in a pout. "It wasn't like that. I was confused. I didn't know what I wanted. But now I do." She reached down and grabbed his hands. "It's you. I want you. Now. Forever."

Nate looked at her, remembering the times they'd had together. He recalled his dad's words about being committed to the ones you loved, putting up with their positive traits and the negatives ones. His dad was the one who'd taught him about doing the honorable thing and not always listening to your heart.

He stepped back but grasped one of Deanna's hands still and pulled her toward a table. Though he'd like nothing more than to show her to the door, he would respect her enough to hear her out. Then he'd explain to her that he was already in love with another woman.

"Let's talk, Deanna."

As Kylie packed her clothes, she wondered about the conversation going on downstairs. The connection she felt with Nate had seemed so real. He wouldn't consider going back to Deanna . . . would he? She paused, holding one of her sweatshirts in midair.

A nudge of doubt lingered in her mind. No matter how well you thought you knew someone, everyone had their own minds to make up. She'd be foolish to be overly certain . . . wouldn't she? She shook her head and placed the last of her clothing into the suitcase.

Moving across the room, she picked up the ceramic mug that she'd purchased with Nate that day he'd played tour guide with her. That was one of the first times she'd seen a new side of Nate, and she'd liked the person she'd spent that day with. Remembering brought a tear to her eyes.

She pulled herself upright and shook her head. She was stronger than this. She'd overcome a lot in her life, and she wasn't going to let insecurity about her relationship with Nate cause her to crumble now.

As she placed the mug into a duffel bag, her mind still lingered on Nate. If she were honest with herself, she'd have to admit that they'd never really spoken about their relationship. They'd acted like a couple but had yet to define what they were.

Based on what Suzy and Darlene had told Kylie, she knew that Deanna had deeply hurt Nate. Kylie knew that Nate liked to stay true to his word—it was why he'd given up his dream career to take over his father's restaurant.

He wouldn't consider another relationship with Deanna while trying to do the noble thing, would he?

Of course not.

But still, doubt lingered in Kylie's mind. The heart was a strange thing.

Maybe Nate had never gotten over Deanna. Maybe this was the moment he'd been waiting for and Kylie had just been someone he'd been interested in on the rebound.

Grabbing her toiletries from the bathroom, she put the last of her things into her suitcase. The truth slammed into her heart—she wasn't ready to leave. There wasn't much about her life in Kentucky that she missed. She wasn't ready to leave Yorktown, and Nate, behind.

Just as she zipped up her suitcase, a knock sounded from downstairs. Probably from the back door. As she opened her apartment door, she heard a familiar voice mingle with Nate's downstairs. She stepped onto the landing and looked down. "Larry?"

Her producer stood at the bottom of the staircase, dressed in his business suit with his hair perfectly combed as always. He stepped toward her when she came into view, but Nate grabbed his arm before he got any closer.

"Kylie! Do you know how worried I've been about you? No phone calls, no emails. You're well past the vacation time you asked for. Some woman even impersonated you at a cooking demonstration at the mall today—at least that's what four people have called to tell me. I've been worried sick."

She slowly walked down the stairs, noting that

Deanna stood close to Nate—too close for comfort —as all eyes were on Kylie.

She cleared her throat and remained where she was. "I emailed you to let you know that I needed to extend my time away. Didn't you receive it?"

Larry put his hands on his hips, his always frantic appearance looking even more frantic and high-strung now. "You think I bought that? Something's going on, Kylie. I thought maybe you'd gone into witness protection or something. Meanwhile, the boss is breathing down my neck about getting some new episodes taped. I told him we haven't even come up with any new recipes lately!"

She sighed and lumbered down the stairs until she stood face-to-face with her producer. "Calm down, Larry. Everything will be fine." Kylie glanced at Nate. "In fact, I was just packing my things so I could return to Kentucky. You can tell the boss not to worry anymore. I just needed some time away."

He grabbed her arm. "Well, your time away is over. I'm taking you back to Kentucky today."

Nate stepped forward. "Wait a minute, buddy. You can take your hand off her."

Nate stared Larry down until he released his grip on Kylie's arm and held up his hands in surrender.

"I'm not trying to cause any trouble. I'm just

trying to save my job and hers." Larry's gaze shot nervously from Nate to Kylie until curiosity replaced the anxiousness. "And just who are you, by the way?"

Nate looked at Kylie. Was he searching her gaze for a response, or was Kylie simply seeing what she wanted to see? "I'm her friend."

Kylie's heart crashed. That was all he was to her. How could she ever have thought there was more to their relationship? They were two people who'd simply let their emotions get the best of them. They'd gotten carried away with the moment and the situation at hand. But at the heart of each of them, their relationship was simply a temporary one.

Kylie cleared her throat, trying to push down her emotions as she turned to Larry. "How'd you know I was here?"

"The producer from Cuisine TV called and asked if I could talk you into taping a special from Yorktown. He said he ran into you at this restaurant where you were working as a waitress. A waitress, Kylie? Of all things I might I have expected, a waitress was not one of them. You're a rising star. If anything, you should have a restaurant with your name on it."

Nate stepped toward them. Kylie could feel his

eyes on her but refused to look up. "Listen, why don't we all sit down for some coffee and talk for a minute. A lot has been going on over the past few days and I don't want anyone making any rash decisions." He paused. "Kylie?"

Against her better judgment, she glanced at him. Nate's eyes implored her . . . but what he was imploring from her, she wasn't sure.

Deanna stepped forward and looped her arm through Nate's. "That sounds like a good idea. Why don't we all talk?"

Kylie had to look away, afraid her resolve would crumble and her emotions would surface all too clearly if Nate saw her eyes again. Instead, she looked at Larry. "Maybe I should just go. Let everyone get on with their normal lives and I can get on with mine."

"Kylie, you can't go yet. We have things to talk about first." Nate's voice sounded gravelly, strained.

"I've heard you have some great new recipes for this place," Deanna said, still touching Nate in a way that made Kylie jealous.

Recipes. Of course that was what Nate wanted to talk about. He probably didn't want to talk about his relationship with Kylie at all. Why would he? He didn't have to explain himself. He'd never made any promises.

"Besides, you heed to eat before you get on the road," Deanna said. "It's dinnertime. I know I'm starving. Nate, do you have any of that Brunswick stew you make that I go crazy for?"

Kylie really wished Deanna would simply stop talking, especially since everything she said and did showed some kind of ownership of Nate and this restaurant. Kylie had never considered herself territorial until this moment. Would it be rude to ask Deanna when she was planning to leave?

"Brunswick stew? That could be a good recipe for your show, Kylie." Larry nodded, as if all for staying a few minutes longer. Kylie knew he probably just wanted a glimpse of the life she'd lived during her absence from the show.

If she refused the meeting too adamantly, she would only look weak. Instead, she nodded. "Fine, let's have dinner." They never had eaten the steak Nate had prepared over at John's place.

They all made their way down the hallway and into the kitchen. Awkwardness fluttered between them, and a knot formed in Kylie's throat. She should have said no and simply gone home. This was not the way she wanted to remember her time here in Yorktown.

"Quaint place you have here." Larry's gaze roamed the kitchen.

"It's ample." Nate stopped by the refrigerator. "Kylie, would you mind helping me while Deanna and Larry go sit in the dining area?"

She shrugged. "Sure thing."

Both Deanna and Larry stayed in the kitchen a moment longer, as if they didn't want to leave. But the look Nate gave them soon sent them scurrying. As soon as they left the kitchen area, Nate turned to Kylie.

Kylie wasn't sure she wanted to hear what he had to say. Instead, she walked to the refrigerator and pulled out some stew they'd made on Friday. As she went to the stove, ready to put it on the burner and warm it up, Nate touched her arm.

"Kylie, we need to talk."

Just feeling his hand against her skin sent shivers up her spine. "There's nothing to say, Nate. It was just . . . we were just . . . a mistake. Now normal life has to resume."

"That's what we were to you?" Anger clouded his eyes. "A mistake?"

"Isn't that all we were to you?" The ache in her throat only got stronger, more painful.

His face softened, as did his voice. "Kylie, don't go yet. Not like this. I want to sit down and talk to you. Really talk to you. More than I can do here in the kitchen with two people waiting for us only feet away."

She grabbed a pot and set it on the stove—a little harder than she intended. "You need to start warming the stew up. It will take a while. I'll put on the bread."

Nate sighed and poured the stew into the pot. He turned the stove top on. "Kylie, Deanna—"

He didn't finish his sentence. The stove exploded. Nate threw Kylie to the ground, his body absorbing the flames that licked the room.

Panic squeezed Kylie's heart.

Was Nate okay? And was this another coincidence or was someone still trying to kill them?

23

That restaurant is apparently one big safety violation." Larry shifted again in the waiting room chair at the hospital. "It's a good thing you won't be there anymore. Next it could be you who's injured. I wonder what their inspection reports are? Probably failed every time. The place is probably just waiting for county inspectors to shut it down."

Kylie pushed back tears, each opinion that Larry freely poured out only adding to her headache and her heartache. She rubbed her temples, wishing desperately that he'd never traveled to Virginia to find her. It was just like Larry to do so, though. "Larry, please stop talking. I just need some quiet right now."

She had to see Nate, to make sure he was okay, but Deanna had insisted on staying with him and Nate hadn't objected. So instead Kylie sat in the waiting room with a grumpy Larry, who more than anything wanted to get on the road and out of this "podunk" town as he'd called it. Kylie had told him he could leave, but assumed he stayed out of some kind of obligation.

"I just can't understand what happened," Kylie whispered, replaying the scene in her head. The stove exploded. A big gas ball hit the air. Nate pushed her out of the way, but the flames caught the bottom of his forearm.

"I thought you didn't want to talk?" Larry said.

As she scowled, Larry chuckled and put his arm around her, pulling her into an awkward hug.

"You just care about everyone, don't you, Kylie?" Larry muttered.

Kylie cared about Nate more than she wanted to admit. But Larry had never been one that she'd talked about her love life with. They had somewhat of a brother-sister relationship, but she'd learned not to mix business with pleasure, if at all possible.

"Even men who just want to rescue you so you can be obedient to them for the rest of their lives," Larry finished.

Kylie pulled away from his embrace. "What does that mean?"

Larry tilted his head in what appeared to be sympathy. "Kylie, it's no secret that you always fall for the control freaks. Seeing the way your family treats you, it's no surprise. Nate sees you as someone who's weak, who needs saving. You can't blame him. He's ex-Coast Guard, right? That's what his old girlfriend was telling me, at least."

Kylie tried to blink back her hurt as the truth crashed onto her, the truth that had been nagging at her since she arrived here but that she'd tried to ignore.

She thought about Nate's career with the Coast Guard. Thought about how her brother talked about sometimes having to choose the people you'd save from a sinking vessel, knowing you wouldn't have time to save them all. So you saved the ones who needed you the most. She thought about Nate's revelation that he still felt guilty over the woman he couldn't save, that he'd vowed to never let that happen again.

Was that what Nate was doing with her and Deanna? Was he simply trying to rescue the woman who needed to be saved the most? Was he still trying to make up for that fateful night when someone had died under his watch and a broken promise?

The realization caused her heart to drop into her stomach.

A relationship built on penance for a past mistake would never last. No, she needed someone who'd love her for who she was. How could she have not seen it earlier?

The door into the E.R. clinical area opened and Kylie sat at attention. A red-eyed Deanna emerged. She barely gave Kylie or Larry a glance before hurrying down the hallway. Kylie stood, knowing she had to check on Nate. He'd saved her life—multiple times—and she at least had to say goodbye, tell him thank-you.

"I have to see if he's okay." Without looking back at Larry, she approached Nate's door, knocking lightly as she did so. A surprisingly strong "Come in" sounded on the other side. She pushed into the room and saw Nate sitting up in bed, his gaze unexpectedly alert.

He smiled when he spotted her. "Kylie. I was hoping it was you and not that grumpy old nurse again."

Kylie tried to smile, but every step she took toward his bed, she contemplated turning back. But she didn't. Her breathing felt labored as she asked, "How are you?"

"First-degree burns. Could be worse."

"Not much." Her heart pounded in her throat as she remembered the moment.

"And the flames only got my arm." He pointed to the bandage on his forearm.

A tear rolled down her cheek. She quickly wiped the moisture away, hoping Nate didn't see it. He must have, because he grabbed her hand.

"Were you worried about me?" His voice sounded surprisingly tender.

Another tear escaped. She chuckled, self-conscious, before looking at him. "You could say that."

"Thank you." His voice sounded low, serious.

She wiped her eyes with her free hand. "Nate, I can't do this anymore."

His eyes widened. "Can't do what?"

"I can't let you play hero with me. You don't really love me. You just love rescuing people."

"Kylie, that's not true—"

She held up her hand. "I'm sorry, Nate. I have to go. John knows you're here and he can pick you up."

Before he could say anything else, she retreated. Larry joined her on the brisk walk to the car. She had no desire to talk as tears spilled down her cheeks.

"You did the right thing, Kylie. You don't want to find yourself in another bad relationship. You've had enough of those." His hand rested awkwardly on her shoulder.

Kylie nodded and wiped at a tear. If she'd just done the right thing, then why did she feel so awful about it? Why couldn't she ever just have a normal relationship?

Larry insisted on stopping for a bite to eat on the way home. Kylie wanted nothing more than to go back to her apartment and get her suitcase and leave this whole place behind. Forget about Nate, the restaurant, her new friends. Instead, she sat stoically through a meal at an Italian restaurant and listened to Larry go on and on about new ideas for her show.

She barely tasted her lasagna or heard Larry, for that matter. This was the right thing to do, right? She and Nate couldn't base their relationship on the events of the past two weeks . . . could they?

When they pulled into the restaurant parking lot, John was there dropping off Nate. Kylie's heart sank. She'd hoped to avoid him for the rest of her stay here.

"You want me to go with you?" Larry asked.

She shook her head. "No, I can handle this alone." Not feeling equipped to handle it at all, she climbed from the car and started toward the back door of the restaurant. Nate waited for her there, his eyes shadowed, his shoulders tense.

"Can we talk?" His voice sounded strained, mellow.

She paused at the bottom step, looked up at him and pulled down in a frown. "I need to get my suitcase."

He stepped down to meet her. "Don't go, Kylie. Not like this. Remember what you said about the restaurant? That if I close it, I need to do it right, not to end on a bad note. I don't want you and me to end like this."

"Was there ever a you and me?" Her voice caught in her throat, the question barely escaping.

"I thought there was." His voice was barely above a whisper. "Kylie, please."

She closed her eyes, fighting exhaustion, weariness and a broken heart. "I can't think right now, Nate. Let me get my bag. I'll . . . I'll talk to you before I leave."

"I'll be downstairs waiting."

She unlocked her apartment and went inside. As she zipped her suitcase and lifted it off the dresser, a paper drifted to the floor. Where had that come from? She didn't remember placing anything on her suitcase before she'd left. Kylie picked it up and stared at the picture on the other side. Realizing what the image was, she gasped.

How had someone gotten a picture of her and Nate at John's house, standing on the balcony and smiling at each other? Who would have done this?

The blood drained from her face.

Her stalker. He'd been in Yorktown. Been in her apartment. The police in Kentucky had arrested the wrong man.

She had to get downstairs. Tell Nate. Call the sheriff.

She spun around and started to run toward the door, but someone wearing black stood in front of it.

24

"*L*arry! You scared me to death." Kylie grabbed her heart and noticed her hands trembled uncontrollably against her shirt. "What are you doing here? How'd you get in here?"

He didn't smile, only shook his head. "I've been there for you through everything. Why don't you ever see me?"

The serious tone of his voice caused a shudder to zip down her spine. She found her voice and tried to steady it. "What are you talking about, Larry? I see you at work all the time."

He shook his head again, his eyes dull, solemn. "No, you never really see me. I've been waiting for you to run to me, but it's always someone else."

Kylie took a step back. "Larry, you're starting to

scare me. I don't understand what you're trying to say."

Nate, please come up and check on me. Please!

Larry took a step toward her, suddenly seeming much more foreboding than before. The businessman had been replaced by someone . . . barbaric. "I've cared about you since before I was your producer."

"I didn't know you before that."

He glowered down at her. "But I knew you. I used to come to all of your cooking demonstrations. You don't think it was just by chance that you got your cooking show, do you? I fought for you. I fought for that show, just so I could work with you, Kylie Summers."

His proclamation caused her heart to stutter. "I had no idea. That's very . . . very flattering, Larry. Thank you for believing in me."

"I wanted to be your hero, the one you turned to. But then you started dating Colin. He treated you like dirt, but you didn't believe it until someone mysteriously sent you emails from the other woman he'd been in contact with. Finally you realized what a jerk he was."

"That was you? You sent those emails?"

"You weren't seeing Colin for who he really was. I

had to do something to make you realize you could do better. I didn't want to see you hurt."

"And you wanted me to do better with you. I had no idea, Larry. You should have told me." Larry was her stalker. How could she have not seen it earlier?

He scowled. "I tried to. Several times. I even asked you on a date before I knew you were dating Colin."

She remembered the day he'd awkwardly come into her office and pulled out a dinner invitation. "I thought you were talking a business dinner. I didn't know you were thinking of it as a date."

Keep him talking, Kylie. Keep him talking.

"I comforted you when you broke up. I gave you a shoulder to cry on. I made you a favorite local TV personality. But you just never saw me in a romantic light, did you Kylie?"

"You should have told me. We could have talked." Her voice trembled.

"Don't placate me, Kylie. You know I'm not your type. I never was. I never will be."

"You're the one who's been stalking me, aren't you?"

He laughed, guttural and devious. "You're just now figuring this out? I thought you were brighter than that."

"But the man they arrested in Kentucky . . ."

"One of your fans. It was so easy. He used to come by the studio every week trying to talk to you. He sent you letters. He called. So I decided to start feeding him information about you, including the time and location of that sting the police set up. Anyone who'd seen you before knew you weren't the one doing the demonstration. Couldn't you have thought of something a little more clever, Kylie?" He touched her hair, and she sucked in a breath. "You're beautiful, you know. I've always known there was something special about you."

"If you think I'm so special, why did you want to scare me so bad? I thought you didn't want to see me hurt."

He shrugged, suddenly looking relaxed and comfortable. "I thought you might run to me. That's all I've ever wanted Kylie—to be your hero."

"There are other ways to be a hero, Larry. I've always thought highly of you."

"I wanted you to need me, Kylie." The dark look returned to his eyes.

Unstable. He was becoming unstable. She had to get Nate's attention or find a weapon to protect herself.

"Larry, don't do something you'll regret."

"I've already done things I should regret. Three times, as a matter of fact. Of course, I don't regret any of them. It sounds so clichéd, but if I can't have you, no one can."

A gasp escaped before she could stop it. "You were the one who tried to run us over? Who pushed me into the water? And the exploding stove—that was for me, too?"

He laughed. "Third time wasn't the charm. In fact, your Prince Charming got it worse than you did. I'm about to change that."

Kylie reached behind her, trying to find something, anything. Nothing. She'd packed up everything. She had to keep him talking.

"Suzy. Larry, did you do something to Suzy?"

His lips cracked in a sadistic smile. "Such a naive little girl. She spotted me taking pictures of you outside the restaurant. I told her you were under investigation by the FBI and I was doing surveillance. The young girl was intrigued. I have that effect on some women. Just not the one I want." His eyes darkened. "I had to keep her quiet, though. She asked too many questions, got too suspicious."

"Please tell me you didn't hurt her, Larry. She didn't do anything."

"You won't be around long enough to find out,

Kylie. I have my own plans for you." He ran a finger down her arm.

"What did you do to her, Larry?"

He scowled. "Don't worry. By the time they find her, we'll be long gone. I gave her a little sleeping medicine and stuck her inside Cornwallis's Cave. The locks were way too easy to pick." He laughed. "Don't worry your pretty little head over her. You should be worried about yourself."

Kylie's throat went dry and her heart beat uncontrollably. "Nate's downstairs. You're not going to get me out of this apartment without him knowing."

Larry laughed. "Don't worry, my dear. I have a plan. I always have a plan."

The last conversation he'd had with Kylie hurt far worse than the bike crash, the water rescue or the oven exploding. What had happened to convince her that he only wanted to save her? And how could he convince her that wasn't true?

The fire marshal waited in the kitchen to review the damage with Nate. The explosion hadn't done as much damage as Nate had feared. He hardly even cared at the moment. All he cared about was talking to Kylie, convincing her to stay here and take over the restaurant. He feared he was too late.

He glanced at his watch, thinking she would have come down by now. As he began walking to the door, Darlene's face appeared on the other side. Her normally cheery expression was gone.

He pulled the door open and she briskly stepped inside.

"Nate, I need to tell you something."

He took her arm and led her to his office. "Okay, Darlene. Go ahead."

She frowned and wrung her hands together. "It's about the man who's been staying at the bed-and-breakfast this week. I went in to clean his room and found a picture of Kylie on the floor. I think Kylie might be in danger."

"Here's what we're going to do," Larry said. "We're going to go downstairs and head back to Kentucky together. If you see Nate and give him any indication that something's wrong, he's dead." He pulled a gun from his jacket, his eyes absent of any compassion or sensibility.

Kylie's gaze traveled to the gun. Her mouth went

dry as she stared at the shiny metal, as she imagined a bullet slicing into Nate's chest. Her entire body shuddered at the thought. Not Nate. If something happened to him because of her, she wouldn't forgive herself.

God, help us.

Larry laughed again and cupped her face with his hand. "It's okay, sweetie. You still have me. I'll always be there for you."

It took everything in her not to flinch, to pull back. *Think, Kylie, think.* She'd survived cancer. Certainly she could beat her producer at this game he was playing with her.

"Larry, we can get you help. You should stop this now."

He dropped his hand and scowled. "There's no turning back now. I've already done enough that if I'm caught, I'll be in jail for the rest of my life. Why stop now?"

"Larry, you can make things right. You don't have to do this."

"I'm just getting started with you, Kylie." He grabbed her arm. "Let's go. We're getting out of here."

"No!" She screamed and thrashed away from him. Her hand smacked against his face. He fumbled backward a couple of steps before righting himself.

"This is no time to get feisty, Kylie." He wiped his lip, saw the blood there and narrowed his eyes. "Don't make this harder than it has to be."

"I'm not going anywhere with you, Larry." She backed up, adrenaline surging through her. Her hands came up in fists, as if she was starting a boxing match. Her breathing was labored, but her eyes focused solely on Larry.

He laughed again and stepped toward her. "Come on, Kylie. Drop the act. You're not a fighter."

"I am a fighter. I've always been a fighter. I just forgot for a while. Never again."

Larry lunged toward her. Kylie knew she couldn't defeat him in a struggle, simply based on the differences in their body sizes. But she could move quickly, use momentum, find a weapon. She had to do something.

Thinking quickly, she ducked. Her leg swung out and hit him in the ankles. Larry lost his balance and stumbled again. She darted toward the door and grabbed the handle. Before she could turn the knob, a hand grabbed her arm and jerked her backward. Pain ripped through her.

"Not so fast." Larry jerked her arms behind her

back. Tears rushed to her eyes as white-hot heat flared through her shoulders.

He pulled some strips of cloth from his sweat-shirt and wrapped it around her wrists. "I tried to do this the easy way. I underestimated you."

The ache going through her bones zapped her power to fight. Larry tied the cloth around her wrists so tightly that she'd already begun to lose the feeling in her fingers.

"You don't think someone's going to see you taking me out of the restaurant? You're not going to get away with this." He pulled his jacket off and threw it over her shoulders, successfully concealing her bound hands. "I'm rushing you to the hospital. You're still not feeling well from your spills yesterday."

He jerked the door open and started to propel Kylie forward. Before he could step out behind her, Nate appeared from around the corner and charged at Larry. The two tumbled to the floor, exchanging blows.

"Kylie, get downstairs and go to Harvey's!" Nate yelled, successfully pinning Larry on the floor. He raised his fist and jabbed Larry on the jaw. Larry groaned, the fight seeming to drain from him.

Kylie remained frozen where she was.

"Go!" Nate ordered.

By the time she got to the bottom of the steps, a sheriff's car pulled up. She stumbled toward it. The deputy caught her before she fell. "Upstairs. My stalker. Nate's in trouble."

The deputy sat her in his car. He darted inside just as another sheriff's car pulled up. It was Detective Blackston.

Kylie pointed toward the beach. "Suzy. She's in Cornwallis's Cave."

Please, Lord, be with Nate and Suzy. Watch over them. Keep them safe.

With surprising strength, Larry pushed Nate off him and rose to his feet. Nate stood quickly, his eyes never leaving Larry. His muscles were rigid and tight as he prepared himself for Larry's next move.

Larry wiped the blood from his lip and stared at Nate with a manic look in his eyes. "You're not going to be her hero this time, Nate."

"It's too late, Larry. Kylie is safe downstairs. The sheriff is on his way. The best thing you can do now is to turn yourself in, to not add anything else to your rap sheet."

Larry laughed and shook his head. "I'm not going to waltz out of here and let you two live happily ever after. No way am I letting you end up with her." He reached behind him and pulled out a gun.

Nate's adrenaline surged. He kept his eyes on the gun, on Larry's finger poised on the trigger.

"I just got your attention, didn't I?"

Nate held up a hand. "Shooting me won't do you any good."

"I'll get the satisfaction of knowing Kylie won't be with you." He laughed again, his eyes becoming glazed. He was losing his grip on reality, if he hadn't already.

"Why do you think Kylie will be with me? She told me earlier that we don't have a future."

Larry shook his head. "Don't play dumb. Kylie looks at you like you hung the moon. She was willing to disappear with me so I wouldn't hurt you."

Nate's heart twisted with concern and love. He'd never want Kylie to put herself in that position, yet it confirmed that she did care about him.

Nate kept his eyes on the gun as he and Larry both paced in a circle. He had to get the weapon away from Larry. All it would take would be one small movement for Larry to end Nate's life.

"I thought you loved Kylie, Larry. Why would you want to hurt her?"

Anger clouded his gaze. "I made her into who she is. All I wanted in return was for her to love me. That wasn't too much to ask, was it? No. But she doesn't want to be with me. She wanted to be with that jerk Colin. I finally got her to see the light with him, and she comes running here and right into your arms."

"You wanted her to run into *your* arms, didn't you? That's why you kept trying to scare her." And it had turned into an obsession. "You know, she did love you, Larry. She told me that you were the one behind the success of her show."

"I was behind the success of her!" Sweat beaded on his upper lip and he waved the gun around. "Kylie was always the selling point. She made the show."

A siren wailed outside. Larry jerked his head toward the sound. Nate saw his opportunity and kicked the gun from Larry's hand. The gun skittered across the floor. While Larry watched it travel out of his grasp, Nate socked him in the jaw. He staggered backward.

Before Larry could gather his bearings, Nate flipped him over and jerked his arms behind him, positioning himself on top of Larry so he couldn't move. Just as he did, the door burst open. A deputy stood in the doorway, ready to take Larry away.

The deputy came downstairs, hauling a handcuffed Larry with him. Nate lumbered behind him, looking as if he'd returned from a war. His eyes lit up when he spotted her and Kylie rose, meeting him halfway.

"Come here." He pulled her beside him, nestling her into his chest with his unharmed arm.

Her head hit his chest. *You shouldn't let him hold you. You can't be together.* But why couldn't she step away either?

"It's okay to cry," he whispered.

She shook her head. "No, it isn't. And it isn't okay for me to be this close to you."

He held her head firmly against him, as if he knew she'd pop it back up at the first opportunity. "Kylie, I want my future to be with you. I know you think I just like rescuing you, but that's only half of the story. You've rescued me, too."

She raised her eyebrows. "Me?"

"You've shown me hope. You've selflessly offered your help and advice at the restaurant—"

"Which I'm pretty sure you resented." Her raised eyebrows knitted together.

"Kylie, you've shown me how good life can be." He shook his head. "I should have told you how I felt about you before today. I kept hoping that the time would never come when you had to leave. I waited too long. I didn't want to tell you how I felt, to influence your decision about whether to stay or go."

"What about Deanna?"

"I just wanted to give Deanna a chance to say whatever was on her mind. And then I wanted to have the chance to tell her that we had no future, that I was already in love with someone else."

Kylie blinked back tears. "You're in love with someone else? Do you really mean it?"

He smiled. "Of course I mean it. Kylie, you are everything I want and need. You're the woman God has been preparing me for my whole life. I don't know what I'd do without you."

She pulled away from Nate enough to dab her eyes with a tissue from her pocket. "You'd be a lot less busy with no one around to save." She tried to laugh but coughed instead as her emotions choked her.

Nate pushed a hair behind her ear. "Don't leave yet. I know it's selfish of me to ask, but stay here. Just a little longer. Long enough that we can figure things out. Long enough that we can figure *us* out."

She didn't hesitate before she nodded. "Okay."

He pulled her toward him. Kylie's arms went around his neck as their lips met in a kiss.

Kylie melted into the moment, finally feeling like everything was right in the world. Her stalker was behind bars. The man she loved, loved her also.

Kylie felt her heart warm and squeezed his hand. She thanked God again for answered prayers.

"I do love you, Kylie."

"I love you, too, Nate."

EPILOGUE

"Hey, beautiful." Nate stepped behind Kylie and slipped his arms around her.

She paused from preparing a sandwich and turned around, leaning against the countertop at The Revolutionary Grill. Nate wrapped his arms around her waist and planted a kiss on her lips.

She smiled and raised her eyebrows. "Is it lunchtime already?" Where had the morning gone?

His eyes sparkled. "Lunchtime couldn't come soon enough."

"What are you talking about? Now that you don't work at the grill, it seems like all you want is to be here. I thought you liked working at the Coast Guard Training Center?"

"I do. But I like seeing you even more, Mrs.

Richardson." He grinned and kissed her again. He'd been able to call her that for the past six months. Kylie still liked the sound of it.

The sounds of people in the dining room filled her ears, and she pushed her sweet husband back some. "I like seeing you, too, but the place is packed out there with a lunch crowd, so I've got lots of food to prepare." She picked up a sandwich she'd made from a new recipe she was playing with. "Here, try this."

Nate took a bite and closed his eyes in pleasure. "Very tasty. I love it." He pulled the bread back. "Is that cranberry sauce, cream cheese and turkey?"

Kylie nodded. "Plus a few herbs. Appropriate for Thanksgiving, huh? I think I'm going to use it on the show this week, and I might even add it to the restaurant menu."

"Everything else you've done for this place has been a hit, so I say go for it."

She glanced at her watch. "The cameraman and producer will be here in a couple of hours. I've got to finish this so I can freshen up."

"You look beautiful . . . as always. And I'm thrilled that you got the restaurant and were able to keep your show."

"I'm thrilled I got to keep you." Kylie kissed him again.

"No hanky-panky back here, you newlyweds."

Harvey, who now worked part-time as a host, pushed through the doors into the kitchen with a huge grin on his face. Suzy and Carrie followed him.

"Just because you two have found love and happiness and have fully embraced your soft sides doesn't mean the rest of us have," Suzy muttered with a smile. "But I am happy for you."

"Thanks, guys." Kylie smiled, amazed at how much they all felt like family to her. "Now, all of you —back to work. We've got a restaurant to run. We're going to put this place on the map."

"I'd say you already have," Harvey said. "We actually have a wait today—at lunch on a Wednesday of all days."

The crew dispersed—except for Nate, who still stood with his arms around her, smiling like a schoolboy. He touched her growing stomach. "What do you think? A chef or a swimmer?"

"We have six more months before we get a glimpse of the little guy. Maybe he'll be a little of both."

"Hopefully he'll have more of you than me."

"I hope he's like his daddy. Honorable, hard-working, a guardian."

"And I hope he's like his mama. You don't even realize how you rescued me from myself."

Kylie grinned. "I guess we both rescued each other, then." She leaned forward and kissed him again, grateful that God had rescued them both.

DEAR READER,

The first time I visited Yorktown and sat in a little beachfront restaurant, I knew I had to set a story there. The quaint town was just too eerie, too steeped in history and too wonderful to pass up.

I enjoyed getting to know Kylie and Nate through writing this story. Each have had things happen in their pasts that affect who they are today—tragedy, painful relationships, cancer. It's easy to hang on to hurts and let them shape us negatively.

Philippians 3:14 tells us that we must press on toward the goal. We must be like runners who keep going, despite the aches and pains along the way. We have to make a choice and let our heartaches and disappointments turn us into better, stronger people.

My prayer is that we can all let go of any hurts in our lives and focus on the bright future we have in Christ.

Blessings,

Christy Barritt

QUESTIONS FOR DISCUSSION

- Kylie admits that it was easier to rely on God in the hard times than it was in the easy times. Some people also feel the opposite—that it's easy to rely on God in the good times and more difficult in the stormy seasons of life. Which do you feel and why?

- What events from your past have shaped you into the person you are today? Have they shaped you positively or negatively?

- Is there anything from your past that you need to reevaluate, that holds you back from your potential? List ways you can let those hurts make you better instead of bitter.

- Nate turned his back on his own dreams in order to let his father's dream live. Have you ever given up your dreams to help someone else fulfill theirs? How did that make you feel? Did you ever regret the decision?

- Kylie feels as if her family babies her. Everyone's upbringing has affected them in some way. How has your upbringing affected who you are today?

- Kylie reflects on life while walking through the historic cemetery. Have you ever taken a walk through a cemetery simply to reflect on life? What do you want people to say about you one day?

- Do you ever feel as if God's not listening to you, that your requests fall on deaf ears? Read Luke 18:1-8. Why can we be confident that God hears us?

- Kylie says she believes in God, but she doesn't need to go to church to show it. Do you agree with this statement? Why or why not?

- Deanna wanted to be in a relationship with Nate because of what he could do for her—potentially give her status or money. Have you ever been in a relationship with someone who appeared to be using you? How did you handle it? What did you learn from the situation?

- Kylie discovers toward the end of the book that you can let circumstances determine who you are, or you can determine who you are through the circumstances. Which one of these notions has been strongest in your life? How can you make changes?

- The townspeople come together amidst the tragedy Nate is facing. When have others been there for you? How does that make you feel? Do you return the sentiment when tragedy happens in the lives of others?

- Do you have any past relationships that have mangled your view of God? A controlling boyfriend? A domineering father? A betrayal by a best friend? How can you let go of those hurts to see a true image of a loving God?